DEAD SERIOUS

Hardy knelt behind a tree and aimed his carbine at the man in the wagon. "Drop your weapons and reach for the treetops."

The two men flinched with surprise, then stiffened as they considered resistance.

"This is a Deputy U.S. Marshal ordering you to drop your weapons."

Both moonshiners looked around, their gaze missing Hardy initially. "Says who?" called the white man with the rifle.

"Says Doyle Hardy, Deputy Marshal, Western District of Arkansas."

"Don't want no trouble with Doyle Hardy," said the black man, pitching his ax to the ground and raising his hands. "He's the son of a bitch that's out to kill his own son."

The white man on the wagon tossed his rifle to the ground. "If he'd do that, he'd kill us as easy as spit."

CHOCTAW TRAIL

WILL CAMP

HarperPaperbacks
A Division of HarperCollins*Publishers*

This is a work of fiction. The characters, incidents, and dialogues are products of the author's imagination and are not to be construed as real. Any resemblance to actual events or persons, living or dead, is entirely coincidental.

HarperPaperbacks   *A Division of* HarperCollins*Publishers*
10 East 53rd Street, New York, N.Y. 10022

Cover illustration by Tony Gabriele

First printing: February 1994

Printed in the United States of America

HarperPaperbacks and colophon are trademarks of HarperCollins*Publishers*

❖ 10 9 8 7 6 5 4 3 2 1

For John Joerschke,
a friend and the editor
who helped me earn a Spur

1

The sun stood midmorning high when Doyle Hardy saw the U.S. marshal approaching along the road from Fort Smith. Straightening from the row of bean sprouts he was thinning and weeding, Hardy planted his hoe at his side and studied Marshal Jacob Yoes for a moment. Even from a distance, Hardy knew the marshal was carrying bad news. Something about the slump of the lawman's shoulders, the low snug of his hat and the stiff set of his hands on the reins revealed the gravity of the message he carried.

Hardy knew the feeling well. He had spent over half of his fifty years as a deputy U.S. marshal riding the Indian Territory and had faced some of the hardest men ever to commit a crime. Men had come at him with guns, knives, axes, trace chains, tree limbs, broken whiskey bottles, fists and even a stick of dynamite once. Hardy had been shot, knifed, clubbed, bruised, slashed and almost blown to bits, but he had survived on instinct. Instinct, though, didn't help a man carry or deliver bad news. Nothing did, save maybe a few shots of whiskey.

After adjusting the suspender strap over his left shoulder, Hardy took his hoe and resumed his garden work. It was a big garden with new beans, potatoes, corn, onions, peas, squash, cucumbers and mustard greens. As many questions sprouted to his mind as plants at his feet. Who among the deputy marshals had been maimed or killed? Why did Jacob Yoes himself decide to deliver the news? After all, Yoes had been one of the two reasons Hardy had turned in his badge. Hardy's son, Bud, had been the other.

At an early age Bud had taken to mischief the way hogs take to slop. Hardy figured his and Bud's trails would one day cross on opposite sides of the law. He didn't want that. Also, Hardy was getting too old for a lawman's life, so he told folks he was retiring due to rheumatism and Marshal Jacob Yoes's infernal set of rules and regulations for deputies in the Western District of Arkansas.

The newly appointed Yoes had titled those rules "Laws Governing U.S. Marshal and His Deputies" and printed them in eight-page pamphlets he had distributed to all deputies. The guidelines permitted a deputy to make arrests for murder, manslaughter, attempted murder, assault with intent to kill or maim, arson, robbery, rape, burglary, larceny, incest, adultery and willfully and maliciously placing obstructions on a railroad track, but limited just how the deputy could go about making those arrests.

Those damn rules made a difficult job harder and dulled a deputy's instincts, making him think twice when a moment's hesitation could mean death—his own. One rule—*No deputy shall ever use the horse or other property of any prisoner in his charge*—stuck in Hardy's craw like a wad of barbed wire. Twice Hardy's horse had been shot from under him and twice he had used prisoners' horses to get back to Fort Smith. Once, even, his own gun had jammed and he had used a prisoner's to kill an attacker and save his own life. Those actions, by Marshal Yoes's strict interpretation of law enforcement, would violate policy. Those regulations infuriated Hardy.

The recollection of those rules sent his blood to boiling and Hardy found himself chopping not just weeds, but bean sprouts as well. He eased off the hoe. Maybe law enforcement was like gardening. For the vegetables to grow and produce, the weeds had to be cut. Otherwise, the weeds would take over and strangle out the vegetables, much like criminals left unchecked by the law would eventually squeeze out the decent folk in Indian Territory.

Hardy glanced down the road as the marshal neared the boundary of Hardy's twenty acres. This wasn't the best soil around Fort Smith, but it was high ground that allowed him to see folks approaching from any direction. That was important to a man who had sent as many vengeful men to prison as he had. Also, the road that passed his place went nowhere in particular. Folks who came down the road were either lost or had business with Doyle Hardy. Marshal Jacob Yoes might be a lot of things, but lost was not one of them.

Behind him Hardy heard the creaking of his front door on thirsty hinges. His wife Tinnie had been on him to oil the hinges, but he had put it off, much as she had put off sharing his bed for so long he had lost track. Though they lived in the same whitewashed box-and-strip house, they shared little more than a roof and his reading glasses, which Hardy knew she used outside his presence to do her needlework and read what little mail she got. The house was simple with her big bedroom up front adjoining the parlor and his smaller room behind hers, connected to the kitchen.

They had married happy and might have remained so had it not been for Boone Dillon, a dapper gambler who passed through Fort Smith and took a liking to Tinnie while Hardy was tracking murderers in The Nations, as Indian Territory was often called. Hardy never once laid an eye on the gambler but what his eyes never saw, his ears heard plenty of through gossip of Tinnie's infatuation with the dashing Dillon. Rumor had it that Tinnie planned to run away with Dillon, but the gambler suddenly up and left Fort Smith. Hardy knew that fellow deputies in each other's absence kept watch on their wives and thought nothing of scaring marital trespassers away. Often, though, Hardy thought it might have been better had Tinnie left with Dillon.

Hardy had hoped the birth of Bud less than a year after Dillon's departure might pull them closer together as man and wife, but Bud had merely replaced Hardy in his wife's affection. In his heart, Hardy was still married to the Tinnie of his wedding day, but in his mind he knew that that Tinnie had died years ago.

"We've got company at the gate," Tinnie called shrilly. "Are you ever gonna oil the hinges?"

"It's the marshal, not company," Hardy replied without looking over his shoulder. "And, you know where the oil tin is."

Tinnie stamped her foot on the porch, then retreated inside to the tune of the squeaking hinges.

Out in the road, Marshal Yoes dismounted and opened the gate in the rail fence. As the marshal entered and closed the gate, Hardy ambled for the corner of his house, leaning the hoe against the whitewashed wall as he passed. He walked with a slight limp from his rheumatism. Hardy lifted his floppy work hat and ran his fingers through his thinning salt-and-pepper hair which matched his bushy mustache and eyebrows. He was two inches shy of six feet tall and a few pounds less than a hundred and sixty. Except for a broad nose, his features were lean and angular.

By contrast the marshal was stocky with a square-set face and a thick head of hair beneath his new felt hat. Yoes had broad shoulders, thin lips and a narrow mind when it came to a deputy's latitude in the field. Hardy supposed him an honest man, even if he was a Republican. Yoes threw out his chest as if to make the badge pinned to his coat lapel even more prominent.

"Morning, Doyle," Yoes offered. "Fine looking garden." His effort at small talk could not mask the gravity of his message.

"They always look good before the summer heat sets in," Hardy replied. He gave the marshal a sly grin. "I appreciate you riding out here to inspect my garden."

Yoes sighed, then took a deep breath. "You know that's not why I came."

Hardy nodded and folded his arms across his chest. Behind him Hardy heard the groaning hinges of the front door.

The marshal let out a slow breath. "There's been trouble in Shacktown, Doyle."

Hardy felt his spirit sag as his arms slid to his side.

Shacktown was where his son lived. "It's Bud, isn't it?"

Yoes bit his lip, then nodded.

"Is he okay?"

"Maybe it's best you just come with me, Doyle. I don't want Tinnie to hear any of this." Yoes dipped his head slightly to tell Hardy that his wife was approaching, then took off his hat and greeted her. "Morning, Miz Hardy."

She answered with a hollow smile as if she didn't care to be addressed by her husband's name. "We don't get many visitors out here, Doyle not having many friends."

Hardy felt his hands knot into fists at her words.

"Can't say about his friends," Yoes replied, "but I know few deputies are as respected in Indian Territory as your husband."

Tinnie snorted. "Care for a cup of coffee?"

"I'd be obliged, ma'am, as long as it don't take too long. I've got to return to Fort Smith directly."

Turning around, Tinnie retreated to the house.

Hardy felt his fists relaxing at her departure. He stood silent until he heard the hinges squeal. "What's wrong in Shacktown?"

"I figure it best you saddle up and go with me. I'd like you to see things for yourself. It's not a pretty sight."

Hardy grimaced. It had to be bad. "Is Bud dead?"

Yoes shrugged. "No, Doyle, but that's all I prefer to say."

With his jaw clenched, Hardy nodded and turned away toward the barn fifty yards behind his house. "I'll saddle up." At the sound of the squeaking hinges, he glanced over his shoulder and saw Tinnie emerging from the house with a tin of coffee for the marshal but nothing for him.

Hardy swallowed the anger as he turned nonchalantly toward the barn. Haste might alert Tinnie to trouble and he didn't want to deal with her questions until he knew the problem. Hardy stopped at the chicken pen and opened the gate so the three dozen hens and pair of roosters could begin their daily foraging about the place.

As he neared the barn, his gray saddle horse and the two plow horses began to dance around the corral, anticipating another feeding. The milch cow stood calmly chewing her cud. Hardy whistled and the gray tossed its head.

Inside the barn the air smelled of fresh manure and old straw as Hardy gathered his saddle, blanket and bridle for the gray. In the far corner, he saw a big rat staring at him. Hardy cursed. Tinnie had a spotted house cat that she wouldn't let come near the barn where it was needed. Instead Tinnie gave the cat the run of the house, pampered her with saucers of milk twice a day. In the evening Tinnie would sit in the rocker on the porch stroking the damn cat's back and ears. Crackers, as Tinnie called the cat, wasn't the smartest cat around, but she had learned one thing—to stay away from Hardy. More than once he'd kicked her out of his way.

Hardy approached the corral gate where his gray stood, waiting to be freed. Hardy stroked the gelding's neck, then gradually slipped the bridle over its head. That done, he opened the gate wide enough for the gelding to exit, then latched it before the team and milch cow tried to get out. Hardy tied the reins to the fence and quickly saddled the gray. After cinching the saddle, he untied the reins and led the horse back to Marshal Yoes.

Yoes finished drinking the coffee and handed the tin to Tinnie. She carried it to the porch, then returned carrying her damned cat just as Hardy reached the marshal. With Crackers cradled in her left arm, Tinnie stroked its neck with her right hand. The cat licked its lips and seemed to grin at Hardy, as if to say she got more of Tinnie's affection than he did.

"Where you going?" Tinnie asked.

"I've business to attend with Marshal Yoes."

"What kind of business?" She stopped stroking the cat's yellow fur for a moment.

"Law business," he replied, walking past her toward the gate and the road.

"Then why aren't you taking your guns?" she demanded.

Hardy ignored the question. "There's a rat in the barn your lazy cat should kill."

Tinnie scowled at Hardy, then wrapped Crackers in both her arms and pulled the worthless animal closer to her. "Crackers tends to the house," Tinnie replied. "The barn is your problem."

"You're my problem," Hardy growled.

Marshal Yoes fell in beside Hardy. Looking over his shoulder, he called to Tinnie. "Thanks for the coffee."

Hardy opened the gate for the marshal, then led his gray through and latched the gate behind him. As he mounted, he saw Tinnie staring hard at him, still cradling that fat and lazy cat like a newborn. Hardy spat at a stone in the road.

Astride his sorrel, the marshal drew up beside Doyle Hardy. Both men nodded and they started the three-mile ride to Fort Smith.

When they were out of sight of Hardy's place, Yoes finally spoke.

"No offense, Doyle, but your wife makes the worst damn coffee I've ever tasted."

"That was my pot of coffee you insulted, Jake. I don't know if her mud is better or worse than mine 'cause it's been years since I tasted any of her coffee or pretty much any of her cooking."

"Why'd you stay with her, Doyle? She never was the same after Boone Dillon passed through Fort Smith."

Hardy pondered the question, uncomfortable discussing it with Yoes. After all, a troubled marriage was no small failure to admit. "I took an oath, for better or worse, and figured I was bound to it."

Yoes clucked his tongue. "You've always been a stickler for oaths, haven't you?"

"I figured my word was about the only thing I had control over." Hardy swallowed hard. "At first I thought I could win her back. By the time I gave up, I figured I just as well make her life as miserable as she was making mine."

Yoes just shook his head.

"And then," continued Hardy, "there was Bud. I thought he might draw us together."

Yoes let out a deep breath. "I figure he'll drive you farther apart before the day's over."

Hardy nodded. "What did he do?"

"Several folks think he killed two people."

"Who?"

Yoes just shook his head. "I want you to see for yourself so you can make your own decision."

"About what?"

"Whether you want to bring him in or you want one of the other deputies to."

"That's another reason I resigned as marshal so I wouldn't have to arrest him, Jake."

The marshal shook his head, more in sympathy than in disagreement. "You may change your mind once we get to Shacktown."

2

The shoed hooves of their horses made a steady clip-clop on the brick of Garrison Avenue as U.S. Marshal Jacob Yoes and Doyle Hardy started down the incline toward the ferry slips on the banks of the Arkansas River. Fort Smith was a bustling town of eleven thousand plus and all the residents seemed to stop what they were doing and stare as Hardy rode past. He sensed everyone but himself knew of Bud's crime in Shacktown.

Fort Smith was a prosperous town that could brag of electric lights, sidewalks, a gasworks, a water-works, two gristmills, three sawmills, a half dozen wagon factories, two furniture manufacturers, two foundries, four newspapers, thirty saloons, a handful of brothels and, most of all, the federal court of Judge Isaac Parker. About the only thing Fort Smith still lacked in 1890 was a wagon bridge across the Arkansas River.

As they passed the side street that ended at the National Cemetery, Hardy saw the grand court building and jail. Through the trees, he could just make out the gallows, which from a distance looked as innocent as a bandstand. Hardy wondered how many more years the gallows would be used to dispense justice for the Indian Territory. Judge Parker was aging, the heavy workload showing in the white of his hair and in the stoop of his walk. Also, outsiders who had never seen the naked brutality of crime in Indian Territory had taken to protesting Parker's brand of justice, calling it Old Testament retribution rather than New Testament compassion. Hardy spat on the clean brick street. The certainty of punishment, not compassion, had made the Indian Territory safer over the past decade and a half, but another ten years of hard justice, not a century of compassion, was still needed to clean up the Indian Territory for good and make it fit for decent humans.

Hardy shook his head as he rode on and the gallows disappeared behind the trees. Was Bud Hardy part of the criminal cancer that needed to be cut off from civilized society? Was Bud destined for the gallows? Where had he gone wrong as a father in raising the boy into manhood?

At the landing a ferry disgorged pedestrians, riders, buggies and wagons from the Cherokee Nation across the river. The passengers were a mixed breed of Cherokees, blacks, whites and all combinations, much like the population of the Cherokee Nation, which occupied the northeast corner of Indian Territory.

Marshal Yoes nodded at a couple deputies who were bringing a half dozen prisoners to jail. Chained to the bed of the wagon that carried them, the six hard men grumbled as they saw the badge on Yoes's coat.

Hardy knew both deputies and, for an instant, they grinned widely at him then seemed to realize something was amiss.

"Sorry about . . . ," one started but was cut off by the marshal.

"Hurry on and get these prisoners to jail," Yoes commanded.

The now solemn-faced deputies nodded.

Even though the marshal and Hardy were among the last in line for the ferry, the tender motioned for them to board first as he collected fares from everyone else. The marshal nudged his sorrel out of line and aimed the horse down the wide wooden ramp.

Hardy followed with his gray gelding and a comment. "Way I figure it, Jake, you just violated your own rules by cutting in ahead of all these other fine folks."

Yoes twisted around and stared wordlessly at Hardy.

Now, Hardy was worried. He had hoped to raise Yoes's dander, but whatever awaited in Shacktown was bad enough a problem that Yoes, ever the stickler for following the rules, wouldn't defend himself against an accusation that surely pricked his conscience. Something smelled as bad as the dead fish along the shore.

At the far end of the ferry, Yoes and Hardy dismounted by the chain that blocked wagons from rolling off the backside into the river. The chain swayed with the gentle rocking of the ferry as Hardy held his reins and stared silently across the river.

Hardy kept mulling over what Bud could possibly have done or who he could have killed. There were

a lot of bad men in the Indian Territory. He hoped
Bud's victims had been that type, not the often
helpless people his kind frequently abused. If anything, Hardy knew he could ask Molina. Molina was
a fine-looking Cherokee woman who had made but
one mistake in her life—marrying Bud Hardy. That
mistake had produced one good result, though, a
bright-eyed boy named Daniel. Barely three, Daniel
was Hardy's only grandson and a bundle of curiosity
and mischief. Hardy wished he saw more of Daniel,
but Bud didn't welcome his father for visits.

Why Molina had ever agreed to marry Bud was
beyond Hardy. Bud was a decent enough looking kid,
but as unpredictable as the weather. Bud, though, had
a charisma that women seemed to find attractive, the
same charisma Hardy had seen in vagabond swindlers
and thieves who could talk honest workingmen out of
their hard-earned money and decent women out of
their virtue.

Hardy knew Molina had tried to make Bud
respectable and had overlooked his frequent dal-
liances with prostitutes. Hardy himself had tried to get
Bud to move with Molina and their son to Fort Smith
and away from Shacktown, a mile upstream from the
ferry landing. That was the final falling out between a
father who was trying to help his son see what was
best and a son who was adamant he was his own boss.
That was six months ago and he hadn't seen Bud nor
his son's family since. By his efforts, though, Hardy
had won Molina's respect and he knew he could trust
her to give an honest answer about Bud, no matter
what the question.

Finally loaded, the ferry edged away from the
bank, the Arkansas's dark waters slapping against
its flat sides, throwing up a mist that felt good

against Hardy's face. As the craft moved away from shore, it gradually left the smell of dying fish along the bank. The odor returned as the ferry neared the far shore, then docked at the slip in Indian Territory. Yoes and Hardy mounted as the ferry crew tied up. When the ferry tender unhooked the chain and dragged it out of the way, Hardy and Yoes rode off.

Yoes immediately put his horse into a canter and Hardy nudged his gray to keep pace. They turned south at the road and galloped toward Shacktown, an amalgamation of poorly constructed log cabins, shanties, tents and hovels built helter-skelter among the trees. As they neared the first house, Yoes and Hardy pulled back on the reins, bringing their mounts to a steady walk. Men squatted in the shade talking to one another or whittling silently. Some chewed tobacco or smoked, but most stopped what they were doing and pointed when Hardy rode by. Then they took to gossiping. The women of Shacktown were gaunt with sunken eyes that hid their looks of fear. Children ran about, bedeviling the many dogs, chasing chickens and avoiding the hogs that roamed the streets scavenging what they could.

At the far side of Shacktown, Hardy saw Bud's cabin. It was no better, but certainly no worse than Shacktown's standard dwelling. Situated on the town's perimeter, the loosely chinked dwelling had an adequate clearing for Daniel's play and little else to distinguish it from the nearby hovels. Hardy hoped to see Daniel out back at play, but instead saw three deputies guarding the place with rifles.

A knot caught in his throat. "Are Molina and Daniel safe?"

Yoes said nothing.

Hardy kicked his gray into a trot and was quickly at the small log cabin. He jumped down from his gelding and looked for a place to tie the reins. Finding none, he tossed the reins to the ground and started for the door.

"Stop him," called Yoes from behind and the three deputies converged at the door to block his way.

Hardy spun around. "What's going on, Jake? Let me inside."

Yoes nodded. "In a minute, Doyle." The marshal dismounted, bent over and grabbed Hardy's reins and handed both sets to a deputy. He let out a big sigh. "It's not a pretty sight, Doyle, but I figured you'd want to see for yourself."

"They're . . . ," the word caught in his throat like a log, ". . . dead, aren't they?" Hardy swallowed hard, then kicked at the ground. "Who did it? Bud? He wouldn't."

Yoes didn't answer for a moment. "That's why I wanted you to see for yourself, Doyle. You can make up your own mind."

Hardy shook his head. "It wasn't Bud."

Yoes shrugged. "We know he's got a mean streak in him after the Rube Bell killing."

"Dammit, Jake," Hardy shot back, "that was self-defense."

The marshal nodded. "I don't deny that, Doyle. But Bud was proud of that killing. Why else would he wear the casing of the fatal bullet on a chain around his neck?"

Hardy had no answer for that. Bud thought killing Rube Bell had made him a man, someone people would have to respect. Hardy knew better. He'd killed a few men in his time. Sometimes they needed it and sometimes Hardy had killed just to protect himself, but never had he boasted of it and never had it brought him respect. He was just doing the job the government paid him to do.

"If you don't want a look, Doyle, I understand," the marshal said. "It's not pretty, but I wanted you to have the chance cause we're gonna have to bring him in."

"Did anybody see him do it?"

Yoes shrugged. "A few folks saw him drinking around the place last night and a couple saw him throwing dice with some other hard cases under a lamp by the river. They said he was splattered with blood and wiping a knife blade on his britches."

Hardy grimaced. "Let's get it over with." He turned from the marshal to the stark cabin.

Yoes nodded at the deputies barring Hardy's way and they stepped aside. Lifting the wooden latch, Yoes pushed the door open.

The odor of death seeped out, reminding Hardy of the smell along the river bank. As Yoes moved inside, Hardy stepped to the door, his eyes adjusting to the dimness. On the dirt floor he saw two lumps— one large and one small, both covered with quilts. As Marshal Yoes lit a lantern in the corner, the room gradually filled with a sickly yellow light.

Immediately, Hardy recognized one of the quilts. It had been given as a wedding present to him and Tinnie by the other deputies' wives. He had been prouder of that quilt than anything but Tinnie on his wedding day. Maybe that was why she had given it away, though he was glad it went to Molina. Around the edges of the quilt, the dirt floor was soaked with splotches of blood. Hardy bent down and studied the blood-stained quilt before picking up a corner and lifting it gently away from the body.

He caught his breath and shook his head. It was Molina, naked except for a pair of cotton stockings and a dress bunched up between her breasts and her waist. She was sprawled on the floor, one hand clutched at her chest like she had been trying to defend herself from the attack and the other knotted on the ground. A look of terror was frozen in her still open eyes because she had been stabbed and sliced in a dozen places. Hardy dropped the quilt because he felt he was violating Molina's privacy.

"I'm sorry, Doyle," Yoes said.

Hardy straightened and moved to the smaller bundle. He squatted again and lifted the quilt from his grandson. Daniel had met death with his eyes shut and a smile upon his face. Were it not for the stab wound to the heart, Hardy might have thought him asleep on the floor. Hardy dropped the blanket and slowly rose, his stomach churning. For a moment, he stood light-headed then marched to the door, stepping outside and taking in a deep draft of fresh air.

In a moment Yoes was at his side. "You okay, Doyle?"

After catching his breath, Hardy shook his head. "How can you be certain it was Bud? He wasn't the best husband, but he wouldn't do this. There are a lot of bad men still in Indian Territory, Jake, the type that would do this."

"You're right, Doyle," the marshal answered calmly, "but we've gone after men with a lot less evidence than we've picked up here. And, there's more. I'm surprised you didn't spot it."

Hardy looked from the ground to Yoes. Hardy knew the marshal was right, knew that Bud was the likely murderer and knew that he didn't want to admit it. That Bud had turned against the very law Hardy had spent his life defending was bitter medicine to swallow.

Yoes clenched his fists. "Can you stand another look at her?"

"If it'll prove Bud was involved."

The marshal turned around, ordered one of the deputies to secure a wagon so they could take Molina and Daniel to the undertaker in Fort Smith. Not twenty yards away, a semicircle of men and curious kids gathered.

Hardy looked at them. "Head on home, all of you."

"You ain't wearing no badge," one replied defiantly.

"But I am," Yoes challenged from the cabin door. "You get home like he says or I will have you arrested."

Begrudgingly, the men and kids began to retreat, murmuring all the way.

Taking a deep breath, Hardy turned around and reentered the cabin. Squatting beside Molina, Yoes pulled the quilt away until it revealed her face and her naked bosom, her right hand knotted across her chest. Hardy looked for a moment, but was unnerved by Molina's dark eyes seeming to watch him from the ground. He bent and gently pushed each eyelid shut. Her flesh was cool and tacky.

"You see what's in her hand?"

Hardy forced himself to look. A blood-covered strand leaked from her clasped fist.

"If this is what I think it is, Doyle, I'd say I'm certain

Bud killed her. I wanted you to be here when I took it from her."

Hardy leaned in closer to the marshal, then studied the strand caked with blood. When he realized it was a necklace chain, Hardy shook his head. If it was what he feared, it would prove to his satisfaction that Bud was a murderer of the worst kind.

Yoes lifted Molina's hand and pried at her fingers, but they were clasped so tightly that the nails had gouged into the flesh of her palms. Gradually, Yoes worked her fingers apart, then jerked the chain from her deathly grasp.

Hardy cringed at the sight of a pendant hanging from the broken and bloodied chain. The chain held a spent .45-caliber casing, the hull from the bullet that had killed Rube Bell. Hardy shot up from his crouch and strode outside. In the struggle for her life, Molina must have jerked it from Bud's neck. Hardy heard Yoes approach. "Bud's our killer and you knew it all along, Jake."

Yoes nodded. "Pretty much suspected it once I saw what I took for the chain. Sorry it had to be this way, Doyle, but I wanted you to see for yourself."

"Have you assigned anyone to bring him in?"

After a long pause, Yoes shook his head. "Knowing you, Doyle, I figured you might want to. Since he's your boy, some of the men didn't want to go after him, fearing they might have to kill him to bring him in. They didn't want to risk that, not with him being your only offspring."

From down the rutted road, one of the deputies returned with a wagon for the bodies.

Hardy shook his head, despising himself for what he knew his decision would be. He had to track down Bud. "I'll go for the boy after Molina and Daniel are buried."

"I'll fill out the papers and swear you in as a deputy tomorrow. You'll have to follow my rules."

Hardy nodded.

"Word we got," Yoes continued, "says he's hiding in Choctaw Nation."

3

Hardy followed the wagon to the ferry, then on into Fort Smith to the undertaker, a slender man with dull, insincere eyes. Hardy instructed him to prepare the bodies, then bring them to his place tomorrow for burial.

As Hardy left the undertaker, Yoes clamped his firm hand on his shoulder, saying nothing, just nodding his sympathy. A crowd, waiting to see the bodies, had gathered around the wagon. The undertaker, following on Hardy's heels, shooed them far enough back that he could gather the blanket-wrapped boy and carry him inside. One bearded fellow moved to lift the quilt from Molina's body.

"Let her rest in peace," Hardy commanded.

Ignoring Hardy, the bearded man grabbed a corner of the quilt.

"Let her rest in peace, dammit," Hardy barked.

With a cockeyed grin on his face, the fellow glanced at Hardy. "Says who?" There was a challenge in his voice.

"Doyle Hardy," the former deputy replied.

The man released the quilt and stepped back. "Yes, sir, Mr. Hardy."

Hardy stood eyeing the spectators, intimidating them by his gaze until no one dared peek at Molina. He stood before them, a silent challenge, until the undertaker returned with an assistant to carry the bundle that had been Molina into the funeral parlor.

Behind him as he mounted and rode away from the undertaker's, Hardy heard the crowd murmuring about him and his son. He departed Fort Smith with his gray gelding at a trot, glad to leave prying eyes behind. Finally alone, he felt his shoulders sag under the horror of what his son had done to his daughter-in-law and to his grandson. His stomach churning, Hardy guided his gray off the road, then dismounted. His cheeks felt flushed and his head seemed to spin. He propped his arm against a tree. His empty stomach began to heave and he bent over to throw up, but there was nothing left from breakfast to release. He stood gagging and choking on the trickle of bitter bile that rose in his throat. In all his years as a law officer, he had never been afflicted like this.

When his stomach spasms finally quit, Hardy crawled back in the saddle and aimed the gray for home. He gave the gelding free rein and lost himself in his thoughts until the horse stopped at the gate to his place. He slid out of the saddle. Opening the gate, he led the horse through, then latched the gate behind.

From the front porch, he heard Tinnie call. "It's Bud, isn't it." There was a panic in her voice. She pushed herself out of the rocking chair, her yellow cat jumping from her lap to the front step, then darting around the side of the house. Tinnie stampeded off the porch toward him.

For a moment, it reminded Hardy of the early days of their marriage when he would return from the Indian Territory and she would run to greet him, flinging her arms around him and kissing him shamelessly. She was still an attractive woman, even at fifty years of age. Her waist was as narrow as he remembered it when they courted and her eyes were just as green, though a dullness had supplanted the liveliness that had first caught his own eye. Her brown hair, though combed in the style of their courtship days and too long for her age, still had a healthy shine to it. Her slender face and high cheekbones still appealed to the man in him. For an instant, he thought she might run all the way to him, throw her arms around him and rekindle the flame of love they had once shared.

But she halted five paces from him and folded her arms across her petite bosom. "It's Bud, isn't it?" By the tone of her voice, she seemed to be blaming her husband instead of her son. "It's Bud, tell me," she scolded.

Hardy jerked the reins of his gray and started along the hard-packed path for the barn.

She fell in step with him, always remaining just out of arm's reach. "It's Bud, isn't it?"

Slowly Hardy shook his head. "It's worse!"

Tinnie stomped her foot and scowled. "Nothing can be worse than something happening to Bud."

Stopping in his tracks, Hardy stared at her. She halted and returned his gaze. Hardy studied her, wanting to gauge her reaction when he told her the bad news. "Molina and Daniel are dead."

Tinnie tapped her foot on the hard-packed path.

Hardy flinched at what he saw. There was no remorse, no glimmer of sorrow, not an ounce of sympathy in her hardened soul. "Did you hear me? Molina and Daniel are dead."

"I heard you. She was a squaw and the boy was a half-breed, so what? Haven't you heard me, I want to know about Bud?"

"The boy was your grandson, Tinnie, and Molina was his mother, for God's sake."

"What about Bud?" she yelled.

His gaze fixed upon the hardness in her eyes and he spat at the ground halfway between them. How could he have ever married a woman this cold and heartless?

"What about Bud?" she screamed.

"He . . . ," Hardy paused, considering how to break the news to her, then deciding to give her an unvarnished blast of the truth to see if it could crack her stone heart, ". . . killed them both, Molina and Daniel."

"Liar," she cried instantly, then rushed at him, her fist upraised. Coming within reach, she swung for his face, but his right hand flew up and caught her puny wrist. She screamed in pain as his fingers closed viselike around her flesh and bone.

Hardy jerked her to himself. "Now listen to me. Our son killed his wife and son. He stabbed her a dozen times, at least, and knifed the boy in the heart. What kind of son did we raise?"

"We?" Tinnie shot back through the pain and anger. "You weren't around to raise him, always out in The Nations tending to other people's problems not your own."

Hardy shoved her away. "You made it clear to me that that was how you preferred it. Things never were right with us after Boone Dillon crossed your trail."

Her eyes narrowed and her lips tightened as if he

had touched a nerve. She pointed her finger like a gun at his nose. "You never did like him."

"Hell, Tinnie, I never even met him, but I heard enough about him to know he was a conniving son of a bitch."

Tinnie lifted her arm to slap him, then thought better of it.

"You were the only one that couldn't see that, Tinnie."

She spun around, her eyes welling with tears, and started for the house.

Hardy grabbed her arm. "I'm gonna care for my horse, then I'm gonna come in and sit down at the table for lunch. You better have something on the table, Tinnie. I don't care if it's cold as long as it's food."

Tinnie shook her arm free and strode to the house, never once looking back. He watched her slam the door in her wake. Shaking his head, he led the gray to the barn, unsaddled him, brushed him down and put out fresh hay.

That done, Hardy took a deep breath and marched to the house, entering through the back door into the kitchen. He was surprised to see Tinnie seated at the table. Arranged in a semicircle around Hardy's plate was a bowl of cold red beans, a platter of cold corn bread, a jug of cane syrup and a glass of buttermilk. It was better than Hardy had been expecting.

Taking his seat opposite Tinnie, he dumped a couple spoonfuls of beans onto his plate, then picked up a slab of corn bread and began to eat. Hardy knew Tinnie didn't want anything to do with him, but she needed to know more about Bud. Hardy ate silently. The beans were as cold as her feelings for him. He avoided looking at her, though he could feel her hot gaze drilling into him. He finished another helping of beans and another corn dodger, then sopped his plate as best he could. With his spoon he cut two more corn dodgers in half, then drowned them with syrup. He took a swig of buttermilk, then drew his sleeve across his mustache.

As he was taking his first bite of corn bread and syrup, Tinnie finally spoke. "How's Bud?" she asked, trying to disguise the venom in her voice.

Hardy glanced up from his plate. "Okay for a murderer."

"He didn't kill them, somebody else did."

Hardy dropped his spoon in his tin plate, lowered his hand from the table and slipped it into his pocket. His fingers wrapped around a .45-caliber hull and a broken necklace chain. Hardy wadded the chain in his hand, then tossed it across the table at his wife. She caught the chain, then threw it to the table. Her eyes widened as she recognized the necklace and her hands flew to her mouth.

"That was in Molina's hand. It's Molina's blood on the chain. How do you explain that, Tinnie?"

"He didn't mean it, not Bud."

Looking up from his plate again, Hardy shook his head slowly. "While ago, Tinnie, you said he didn't do it. Now you're saying he didn't mean it. Which is it, Tinnie?"

Her lips quivered and she buried her face in her hands to sob.

"Which is it, Tinnie?"

"I don't know," she mumbled through her palms.

"There's a hell of a lot you don't know about our son, Tinnie. He's got a mean streak in him that I never understood, unless you meant to turn him against me."

Through her fingers, Tinnie peeked with red-rimmed eyes.

Hardy finished eating his syrup and corn bread, then downed the rest of the buttermilk. Reaching across the table, he grabbed Bud's necklace, then stood up and shoved it back in his pocket.

"Where are you going?" she demanded.

"To dig a couple graves."

Tinnie slapped her hands against the table and shoved herself up, knocking her chair over behind her. She planted her hands on her hips. "Don't bury that squaw and half-breed boy on my place."

"I always thought it was our place, Tinnie, or maybe my place. I'm the one that does all the work. I can't even get you to fix me a hot meal, though you'll fix that damned cat a saucer of milk every time it whines."

In bewilderment she ran her fingers through her hair. "Squaw and half-breed," she cried. "Bud deserved better."

"And they deserved to live." Hardy spun around and strode out the back door, heading for the barn. He heard her step outside onto the porch, knowing she was curious where he planned to dig the graves. He aimed for the toolshed where he grabbed his shovel and grubbing hoe, then retreated for an oak tree at the back corner of his place. It was a peaceful spot, quiet and away from the road, where the occasional traffic would not disturb the eternal sleep of mother and child. Hardy glanced up at the sky, gauging he had about four and a half hours until sundown to finish the graves. As he started digging, he saw Tinnie retreat inside the house.

Thanks to plentiful spring rains, the ground was soft and the work easy in spite of the oak tree roots he encountered. The labor helped him work away his anger, much as it had helped him deal with the frustrations of being married to a cold woman.

After an hour, he glimpsed Tinnie at the chicken coop collecting eggs, then chasing the chickens back to the pen. He could not remember the last time she had helped like that. It surprised him even more when she caught an old hen, tied her up to the clothes line, whacked her head off with a knife and let the blood drain. Later, Hardy saw her plucking and gutting the chicken.

Her activity so surprised him that it slowed his work. He dug one grave wide enough for two coffins. He made the earthen walls straight and square. This was the last thing he would ever do for his daughter-in-law and grandson, so he would do it right. The sun had disappeared behind the trees and the grave had fallen dark and murky as death before Hardy was satisfied with his neck-deep hole. He notched a couple footholds in one corner of the grave, then threw the shovel and grubbing hoe out before pulling himself out. As he walked to the house, he was surprised to see a light in the kitchen and a plume of smoke boiling out of the stovepipe.

At the kitchen door, he pulled off his muddy boots, then his dirty trousers and shirt, piling them in a washtub by the back. He entered the kitchen wearing nothing but his socks and his union suit and was surprise to see a supper unlike any he had seen in months on Tinnie's kitchen table. She had prepared fried chicken, boiled potatoes, deviled eggs, her own canned black-eyed peas, store-bought canned tomatoes and dried apple cobbler. On top of that, she had pulled into the kitchen the big tub they used for bathing and was boiling water on the stove for his bath.

He was even more surprised when Tinnie entered the room. She had combed her hair and tied it with a bow. She had rouged her cheeks and colored her lips as well. She offered him a hollow smile and motioned for him to sit down at his plate. Maybe it was wrong of him, but rather than being grateful for this, Hardy was suspicious. What was she up to?

As Hardy slipped into his chair, Tinnie pulled out a tin of fresh biscuits from the oven and placed them on the table. When she was seated, Hardy began to help himself. He ate a generous meal, knowing that food would be scarce once he took up his son's trail in Choctaw Nation. Not a word was said between husband and wife until he had finished his final biscuit then started on a bowl of cobbler.

"You're going after him, aren't you?"

Hardy nodded.

"He didn't mean to do it. Just let him go."

Hardy shook his head. "Can't do that."

"Let the deputies do it. He's smart enough to get away from them, but not from you."

Hardy shook his head again. "Nothing you can do will change my mind, Tinnie." He watched twin tears roll down her cheeks. It was too late for crying, years too late.

Tinnie lost her appetite and disappeared into her bedroom while Hardy finished a second bowl of cobbler. Standing up and stretching, he went to the stove and grabbed a couple of hot pads to pour the pot of boiling water into the washtub Tinnie had already half filled. Then Hardy stripped and began to bathe in the warm water.

When he was done, he dried himself with a towel Tinnie had draped over the back of the chair, then pulled on a clean union suit she had placed on the chair's seat. Hardy carried the lamp from the kitchen to his bedroom, catching a glimpse of Tinnie sprawled across her bed in her own darkened room.

Hardy squatted down by his bed and pulled out a long narrow crate that he had hinged and made into a trunk. This was where he stored his pistol and carbine as well as the other accoutrements of the lawman's trade. He lifted the trunk and dropped it atop his mattress to gather the things he would need tomorrow. As he was removing his pistol and holster, he heard a shuffling at the door into Tinnie's room.

She stood before him naked, still a striking woman at her age.

He bit his lip.

"If you'll stay and leave Bud alone, I can make things right between us," she offered.

"It's too late for that and it's too late for Bud," he replied.

Tinnie retreated to her room and sobbed well after Hardy had organized his things and fallen into bed.

4

The small group, made up mostly of deputies and their wives, clustered around the open grave which cradled the coffins of an adult and a child. A long-legged, long-winded preacher droned on about the unfairness of death in taking a mother and child so young. When the preacher finally called for a prayer, all bowed their heads except Hardy. He surveyed the crowd, noting Marshal Jacob Yoes and several of the deputies with their somber-eyed and obedient wives.

Presence of the wives made it all the more embarrassing to Hardy that Tinnie had refused to attend the simple service. She had closed herself up in her bedroom and spurned Hardy's every plea for her to join him. Why should he have been surprised? She had dismissed so many of his suggestions and advances over the years that it had become second nature to her. To the arriving mourners, Hardy had apologized for Tinnie's absence, claiming she was just too distraught to handle the deaths of her only grandson and his mother.

When the preacher said "amen" he was the first in line to extend his hand and his sincere condolences. Hardy shook his hand, then released it, but the preacher just stood there smiling, the palm of his hand still up. Hardy fished a couple coins out of his pocket and dropped them in the preacher's hand without even checking their value. The preacher seemed satisfied and walked away toward the mule he had ridden to the service. The undertaker was next in line, telling Hardy he had washed both mother and child and dressed them well before placing them in the coffin. The undertaker leaned close to Hardy, as if to tell him something intimate about the deceased.

"You'll be getting the bill," he whispered. "Do you want me to add a couple tombstones to it?"

Hardy shook his head. "Can't afford it right now."

The undertaker gave his first truly sorrowful look since he arrived driving the hearse. He retreated in disappointment.

As the women lined up to give their condolences, a couple of the deputies retrieved the shovels they had brought and began to cover the coffins. Grabbing Hardy's shovel, Marshal Jacob Yoes helped.

The passing women hugged Doyle, expressing their horror at the tragedy and sympathy for Tinnie. To each one, Hardy nodded. "She was too devastated to handle the burial."

"We brought food for you," one of the women said.

Hardy thanked her. "Just leave it on the front porch by the door and I'll carry it in."

"We don't mind taking it in for you."

"Tinnie still being in a fragile frame of mind, it's probably best that I do it." After last night, Hardy wondered if Tinnie had ever gotten dressed. "You do understand, don't you?"

"I just hope she's okay while you're out in The Nations."

"She'll do fine."

After the women, the men passed by one by one, saying little, just nodding with clenched jaws and drawn lips. Mostly lawmen, they knew what faced Hardy in Choctaw Nation.

"You be careful," one of them said.

With several men alternating on the shovels, the grave was quickly covered and mounded over. That done, most of the men edged toward their mounts or buggies to help the women carry food to the front porch.

The marshal was the last one to approach Hardy. From the pocket of his broadcloth coat, Yoes pulled out the badge of a deputy U.S. marshal. "You sure you want to go through with this, Doyle?"

Hardy nodded.

"You'll be expected to follow my rules for deputy marshals."

Hardy nodded again.

Yoes stepped up to Hardy and pinned the badge on Doyle's coat.

Hardy lifted his hand to take the oath.

"You've sworn to it once, Doyle Hardy. With you that's enough." The marshal pulled an eight-page rules pamphlet from his pocket and shoved it into Hardy's hand. "That's what I expect from you or any other deputy, no exceptions." Then Yoes extracted another piece of paper from his coat pocket. Hardy recognized it as a warrant. "Here's the papers on Bud." The marshal held the warrant close to his chest rather than giving it to Hardy. "I've played it over in my mind a hundred times, Doyle, whether to let you go after your boy or not. I figure you'd try to bring him in alive, more so than any other deputy, though I'm not entirely certain of that."

Shrugging, Hardy stared the marshal hard in the eyes. "He'll be treated like any other criminal."

"Accused criminal," Yoes corrected.

"Whatever you say, Marshal." Hardy reached and pulled the papers from Yoes's fingers.

"You remember deputy fees, don't you?" Yoes asked, then delineated them in spite of Hardy's nod. "Six cents a mile on official business, a dollar a day expenses and fifty cents for serving papers. Two dollars an arrest—I figure you'll just make one—and seventy-five cents a day to feed your prisoner. If he's killed, you don't get his food money."

Hardy tucked the warrant and Yoes's set of rules in an inside pocket of his coat. "I'm saddled up and as soon as I tend to Tinnie I'll be leaving, Jake."

"How's Tinnie?"

"She seems touched in the head by it all, but like you said, she ain't been the same for years."

Yoes lifted his hat and snugged it down over his head. "You be careful out in The Nations. Word's gotten out, I'm sure, that you'll be riding the territory looking for Bud. There's bound to be a few fellows who think now's the time to settle the score for some past grievances. You remember the LeHew brothers were let out of prison a few months back?"

"Yep," Hardy answered, "about the time I resigned."

Yoes shook his head. "Last they were seen was in Choctaw Nation. Word is they want your skin for sending them to prison."

Hardy shrugged. "I've been able to hold my own

against those types in the past, though I didn't have to follow your picky rules."

"We've all got to follow rules." Yoes scratched his chin.

Hardy turned for the house, but felt Yoes's strong hand upon his shoulder.

"I don't know if I'm doing the right thing by you and your boy." Yoes let his hand slide off Hardy's shoulder. His face was clouded with doubt.

Shaking his head, Hardy sighed. "I'm not sure I'm doing the right thing either, Jake. I'd have let another deputy go after him had he not killed his own flesh and blood." Hardy paused to stare at the marshal, then admitted what he had told no other person. "I feared it might come to this with Bud. I didn't want to have to arrest him for his crimes, that's why I resigned as deputy."

Yoes nodded slightly. "I always took it that I was the reason you quit, especially after I offered you reappointment. You're one of the best in this line of work, Doyle, and it didn't help my reputation, you resigning."

Hardy nodded. "I've never been one for all your damned rules, Jake, and I've been up front about that, but I never had anything against you personally. It was Bud I didn't want to face, not because I feared him . . ."

"You never feared anybody."

". . . I just didn't want to have to kill him." Hardy offered Yoes his hand.

The marshal shook it firmly, sealing a common bond of respect between men whose politics differed and whose views varied on doing a marshal's job. As their hands broke apart, they said nothing more and walked side by side toward the house.

Hardy saw women depositing the final baskets, dishes and pots of food on the porch before joining their men for the return to Fort Smith.

"Good luck in the Choctaw Nation," Yoes said a final time, then angled for his sorrel mount.

Hardy stood alone as the string of mourners circled their rigs and horses about and began the trip back to Fort Smith. As he turned around, Hardy thought he saw a curtain move in the front window. Tinnie!

Marching to the house and up onto the porch, he saw Tinnie's yellow cat sniffing at a basket of food. He swung his boot at Crackers, but the cat scurried around the corner. "There's a rat in the barn if you're hungry," he scowled. Bending by the door, he grabbed the basket, then slid the handle up his arm before picking up a couple of cloth-covered dishes. Despite loaded hands, he managed to open the front door, its dry hinges squeaking for oil. As the door swung open, Tinnie was standing to the side, dressed in black, even wearing a veil over her face.

"Finally decided to mourn your lost grandson?" he asked as he strode past her on the way to the kitchen. The table was still cluttered with last night's dishes and leftovers. The tub where Hardy had taken a bath was filled with gray soapy water as cold as her heart.

He heard Tinnie shuffle into the kitchen behind him. "I'm mourning for Bud, my son."

Hardy sneered at the absurdity. "Bud ain't dead."

Tinnie stared at him, her eyes wide, her lips quivering like leaves in the breeze. "He's as good as dead once you walk out of this place."

Hardy placed the dishes on a clear spot on the table, then slid the basket off his arm into a chair seat.

"I intend to bring Bud in, not kill him. It'll be up to the judge and jury to hang him."

"You'll testify against him."

"I'll testify to what I saw and found." He remembered Bud's bullet-hull necklace and retreated to the back porch where he fished it from the britches he had worn to dig the grave. He shoved it in his pocket, then strode through the house for another load of food. Tinnie just stood and watched, never offering to help or so much as move out of his way on the final two trips.

It was nearing noon so Hardy decided to make a meal of folks' generosity. He went to the wall shelf and fetched a tin plate, then began browsing through the gift dishes. He grabbed the fork he had used last night and stabbed a half dozen slices of roast beef from one pot, then scooped some hominy from another and a couple halves of baked squash from a pie tin. The basket held two loaves of baked bread and he grabbed one loaf and tore it in half, then bit into it ravenously. He hadn't fixed himself any breakfast, spending his time instead saddling his gray and dressing for the funeral. As soon as he finished this meal, he would be heading west.

He slid into his chair and began to eat. Tinnie walked around the table, seemingly in a trance, finally stopping to stare at him.

"Don't go after Bud," she pleaded. "He's my son. He's all I've got left."

"What about me?" Hardy asked sarcastically.

She flew into a rage, sweeping her arm across the table, knocking dishes and utensils to the floor. She grabbed a carving knife and flashed it over her head. "You don't understand, he's all I've got left. I'll kill myself if you leave."

Hardy continued eating.

"Do you hear me?" Tinnie shouted.

Hardy nodded. "I heard you. I told folks you were crazy with grief. No one would be surprised if you gutted yourself."

She threw the knife on the table in exasperation. "What other lies did you tell them? I didn't want that squaw and half-breed kid buried on my place."

"Our place," Hardy corrected.

"Bud was better than her, could've done much better for a wife than Molina."

Hardy pointed his fork at Tinnie, his voice taking a dangerous tone that stopped Tinnie's rambling. "Molina was better than Bud, a hundred times better. She had a decent streak in her and made him a good wife. She deserved better than a cabin in Shacktown. And the boy . . ."

Tinnie crossed her arms over her chest and thrust out her chin. "I've heard how those squaws are. Who's to say the boy was actually Bud's."

"Some people, Tinnie, say the same thing about me and Bud."

Tinnie screamed and lunged across the table for Hardy, flailing her arms and kicking her feet as she broke dishes and spilled food all over the floor.

Reacting quickly, Hardy shoved her head aside, then jumped up and grabbed a half loaf of bread before she could fling any food on his clothes. Having taken all the abuse he could stand, he retreated to the parlor and grabbed his hat. He pulled it over his head and jerked open the groaning front door.

"Don't hurt my son," she screamed from the kitchen.

"Our son," he corrected, then slammed the door behind him.

He moved quickly to the barn and his gray. The gun belt he had draped around his saddle horn he retrieved and fitted around his waist. He gave a final check of his carbine, bedroll and saddlebag stuffed with supplies and ammunition. With the loaf of bread in his hand, he mounted and rode to the front gate, bending over in the saddle until he could lift the latch. He let himself out, then closed the gate.

On the road, he touched his heel to the gray's side and the gelding galloped away from his place and toward Choctaw Nation.

The sky was turning pink around the edges
when Deputy Marshal Doyle Hardy neared
Skullyville, a slight town southwest of Fort
Smith and five miles south of the Shallow Rock landing on the Arkansas River. At one time, Skullyville
had been the first stage stop west of Fort Smith on the
old Butterfield Stage Line, but those days were long
gone. The town had never full recovered from the
Civil War when several buildings were burned. Now it
was a modest town with a few stores serving the traffic
on the Fort Smith-Boggy Depot road.

Once he crossed the line from Arkansas into
Choctaw Nation, Doyle Hardy felt truly free for the
first time since his retirement. He had left Tinnie and
all her problems behind. His spirit rose. Tinnie had
forced him to forget what freedom had really been.
Now he remembered and liked it.

And too, there was something about hunting a
man. It was unpredictable, drawing on a deputy's
every skill of intuition, doggedness and desire, not to
mention just plain hard work. The hunt was the fasci-

41

nating part of law enforcement, the capture a mere sideshow and the return to jail pure drudgery.

Hardy tried to forget that his quarry was his own son, his own flesh and blood. Occasionally as Hardy rode along, his thoughts put themselves into words which he mouthed unintentionally. "Why, Bud, why?" he found himself repeating from time to time. A wise fugitive would head straight for the Red River and cross into Texas as soon as possible. A wiser or less cocky fugitive might have eschewed the well-traveled Fort Smith-Boggy Depot Road, but Bud was neither. Hardy knew, too, that Bud frequented brothels and likely would spend more nights in a prostitute's bed than on the trail. Hardy just hoped Bud didn't fly into a murderous rage and kill another innocent woman.

Periodically, Hardy took bites from what was left of the half loaf of bread he had brought with him. The bread lasted until he approached Skullyville at dusk. Lamps were being lit in the cabins as he reached the outskirts of town. He tugged his hat down low and rode along the hard-packed road that split the town in half. Arriving at this time of day, Hardy figured to reduce his chances of being recognized, but he had barely reached the center of town when he heard his name called.

"Doyle Hardy, Doyle Hardy," shouted a man intent upon alerting the entire community of his arrival.

The commotion was generated by a slight, dark-skinned man Hardy recognized as Kirby Sands, a member of the Choctaw police, who operated under their own set of laws as determined by the Choctaw Nation's constitution. Why didn't Kirby produce a brass band and fireworks to announce Hardy's arrival as well? Hardy drew up his horse, waiting for Kirby's approach and hoping the excitable Choctaw wouldn't wake up the dead. Kirby was an honest, decent type of Choctaw, like most of his people who tried to carve out a peaceful existence in life. As a Choctaw lawman, Kirby was authorized to enforce the Choctaw law among his people. Any time a crime was committed by a Choctaw against a Choctaw in Choctaw Nation, it was resolved by Choctaw law and Choctaw police. However, when a white man committed a crime against a Choctaw, the jurisdiction fell under the court of Isaac Parker and the U.S. Marshal's Office.

Hardy bent low over his horse and rested his hands on his saddle horn as Sands ran to his side. Before Sands could say anything more, Hardy growled. "Can you yell any louder, Kirby, so everybody in Choctaw Nation will know I'm around?"

Sands flashed a wide grin, his full set of teeth practically glowing in the dimness. "I guess I got a bit excited," he said, taking off his hat with an eagle feather in the band. "It's no secret that you're in Choctaw Nation or who you're after. That's why I needed to talk to you."

Hardy nodded. "Let's talk somewhere not so public, Kirby."

"Where you staying the night? I can put you up in a bed."

"I best get accustomed to sleeping on the ground again, Kirby. Meet me in an hour down by Rock Spring."

"Sure thing," Sands replied, plopping his hat atop his head, "but you need to know I'm not the only one that knows you're back in these parts."

Certainly not now, Hardy thought. With Sands's loud greeting, probably every man within firing range knew of Hardy's arrival. Hardy nudged the gelding and the gray started moving again. Hardy walked the horse through town, trying to bring no more attention to himself than Sands had already done. No one else seemed to take an interest in him, yet Hardy knew everyone saw him and word of his manhunt would spread throughout Choctaw Nation. One thing Hardy never understood was how news could spread so quickly among a people who didn't rely on the telegraph. From his years of riding the trails of The Nations, Hardy seldom hunted an outlaw who didn't know who was following him. It just seemed that news traveled faster than lightning in Choctaw Nation.

In the gathering darkness a quarter of mile from town, Hardy could just make out the trace that led to Rock Spring. It was one of numerous perennial springs that surrounded Skullyville. The spring bubbled cool water like the others, but nature had made this one a lawman's favorite by surrounding it with big boulders that provided a natural fortress.

The cool breath of night sent the tall pines to murmuring among themselves as Hardy turned off the road and aimed his gray down the narrow trace. Up ahead Hardy heard the startled retreat of animals, likely deer, running from his approach. A couple crows squawked then flew from a tree as Hardy passed. About a hundred yards from the road, Hardy was just able to make out the rounded shapes of the boulders ringing Rock Spring.

"Rider coming in for water," he called softly in case anyone else had taken camp there for the night. Only the rustling of the trees answered him.

The gray had been here before and seemed to remember the trail that snaked among the rocks, then stopped at a small sloping meadow that was boggy down slope from the spring, but firm and grassy up slope. The gray swung wide of the soft wet ground and headed instinctively up slope where Hardy dismounted. Taking hobbles from his saddlebag, he worked them over the gelding's hooves, then removed his bedroll, saddlebags, carbine and saddle, stacking them all against the base of a head-high boulder. He jerked the saddle blanket off and then removed the gray's bridle, taking a little time to stroke the horse's neck before letting it graze and water.

Hardy draped the saddle blanket over a small rock to dry from the horse's perspiration, then unrolled his bed, using his saddle as a pillow. He tossed his hat aside and loosened the tie he had worn since the burial that morning. He walked around, working the kinks out of his legs, knowing they would be stiff in the morning. His legs seemed to tighten up on him more than he remembered. Was it just the four-month hiatus since he had ridden The Nations or was his age finally catching up with him?

Finally, he sat down on a rock and massaged his legs, trying to improve the circulation and his confidence in them. At the call of the approaching Kirby Sands, Hardy stood up. Despite all the attention, his legs had stiffened on him. He limped to his bedroll, kicking at the grass in frustration. Hardy answered, "Come on in."

Shortly, he made out Kirby Sands's approaching form. The Choctaw lawman had walked rather than ridden over. He made his way among the boulders and stood opposite Hardy. Though he couldn't see Sands's expression, he saw the bobbing of his hat as he nodded.

"All the law-abiding folks are glad to have you back in Choctaw Nation," Sands said, extending his hand which Hardy grasped and shook. "Some of the bad men are glad, too. Gives them a chance to settle old scores."

Pulling his hand from Sands's, Hardy shook his head. Why did it have to get any more complicated than it already was? "What men?"

"The LeHew brothers have been talking big about getting you before you reach Boggy Depot."

Hardy cursed. "Who said I was going to Boggy Depot?"

"The wind," Sands replied. "Who knows how news travels in Choctaw Nation? I've just always blamed the wind."

"Who else has the wind told about my return to Choctaw Nation?"

"Flem Thurman for one."

Hardy scratched his head. "That's one I don't recall."

"He's an old man, your age or older," Sands started.

Were it not for the cramps in his legs and the aches in his joints, Hardy might have argued whether he was a fossil or not. "Old like me?" Hardy asked.

"Yep," Sands replied, then continued without ever realizing his mild insult. "He just finished five years in prison."

Hardy shook his head. "Don't remember anything about him. Why doesn't the wind speak to me like it does everyone else?"

"Somebody else got him convicted for whiskey running or horse thieving."

"Then why the hell's he after me, Kirby?"

"While he was in prison, you killed his boy down along the Kiamichi River."

Hardy pinched the bridge of his nose. Now it began to make sense. He recalled the incident four years ago. He was chasing a whiskey peddler who happened to run into Elroy Thurman between Kiamichi Mountain and Winding Stair Mountain. Thurman had killed and robbed the peddler of a thousand plus dollars, little knowing that the law was less than a half mile behind. Thurman was still looting the peddler's body and celebrating when Hardy rode up. The gloating ended when Hardy commanded him to throw up his hands. The last mistake Elroy Thurman ever made was grabbing for his pistol.

"Damn shame so many bad men have kinfolks, Kirby. Any idea what Flem Thurman looks like and where he stays?"

"I saw him once in town. Toothless fellow with big drooping jowls, wears overalls and carries a short-barreled shotgun. He's supposed to have a cabin near the road about ten miles down the Old Boggy road from here, near the old Atoka place. You know that fine house the Atokas built before they was killed? Well, a hussy called Kitten's turned it into a play house for traveling men."

This was the type of information which could help Hardy stay alive. "You heard about any others that may be looking for me?"

"Nope," Sands replied.

"You know who I'm tailing?"

The Choctaw lawman stood silent for a moment. "The wind says it's your boy."

"The wind is right," Hardy replied.

Sands clucked his tongue. "Sorry it's true. I heard that Bud passed through town yesterday. I didn't see him, but some said he was spreading word you'd be following him. That may be how Flem Thurman found out. What'd Bud do that got you on him?"

"Knifed his wife and boy."

Sands clucked his tongue again. "That don't sound like the doings of a Hardy, not someone out of your stock."

Hardy could only shake his head. "Wish it weren't so, Kirby, but afraid it is."

"Life ain't always fair," Sands replied.

There was nothing more Hardy could say about Bud. He didn't like talking about his boy's crime. It brought back the horrible vision of Molina naked and bloodied and little Daniel, his chest punctured.

"Thanks for coming out, Kirby, and for the good information."

"Me and my people owe you, Doyle, for making Choctaw Nation safer."

Nodding, Hardy considered chiding Sands for calling out his name on the street of Skullyville, then decided against it. Sands was a good man who was doing more than his part to keep law in Choctaw Nation. "Take care, my friend."

"And I'll look for you on the return trip. You're always welcome to stay with me and my family any time."

Hardy laughed. "As many men as are carrying grudges for me, I wouldn't want to put your family in danger."

"You're still welcome, just the same." Sands tipped his hat to Hardy, then turned around and slipped from among the boulders so quietly that Hardy's gelding never fidgeted or lifted his head from grazing.

Hardy limped over to the horse, fighting his aches and rheumatism with every step, and double-checked the hobbles. They were secure. Hardy eased over to the spring, squatted down and cupped his hand to his lips, enjoying the cool sweetness of the spring water.

Standing up, Hardy listened to the whispering of the pines in the breeze. The full dark of the moonless sky was broken only by the stars which were but pinpoints of light in an otherwise blackened sky.

Though he wasn't sleepy, there was nothing else to do but retire, so he unfastened his gun belt and put it by his saddle where he could get it more easily if he needed it. Removing his tie, he slipped it in the coat pocket that held the warrant for Bud and the marshal's infernal rules. Pulling off his coat and folding it in half, he laid it over the seat of his saddle.

After pulling off his boots, he slid his aching legs beneath the top blanket of his bedroll and awaited sleep. Rest was long in coming and fitful when it arrived, the bloodied images of Molina and Daniel floating through his dreams.

6

Two hours after sunup Doyle Hardy topped the final rise before the old Atoka place. Reining up the gray, he shook his head at the overgrown fields, the barn in disrepair and the house with peeling paint. The place had deteriorated badly. Outside three horses were tied to a hitching post, likely the mounts of late-sleeping customers. Out back two more horses pranced nervously around a small corral. Whatever the place had become, it was no longer a farm.

The house looked dilapidated, its shutters askew, its roof sagging from needed repair. Three years ago the farm had been a fine place with as good a house as could be found in these parts, a new barn and a newly planted crop just pushing its way through the spring soil. But before the crop stood a foot tall, the whole family—the parents and five kids—had been murdered by a Choctaw who went crazy on a batch of bad whiskey. It was a Choctaw matter, handled by Choctaw police and Choctaw courts. The murderer, a handsome Indian who had never been in trouble before, was convicted and sentenced to die by a single bullet to the heart. Simeon Silon had taken the verdict without flinching, merely asking that he be set free until his execution date. He gave his word he would return to the appointed place at the appointed time and by Choctaw law he was set free.

Though he had weeks to escape before his execution date, Simeon Silon returned to his home and his work as if he had never committed such a horrible crime. Though his wife and parents pleaded with him to escape, Simeon Silon told them he had given his word and that was all he had left since committing the horrendous murders. He might die as a murderer but at least he would die as a man of his word.

Hardy had arrived at the execution site the day before the appointed date as the U.S. Marshal's official representative. A lot of men were taking bets whether Simeon Silon would show up or whether he had made fools of Choctaw law. There was a lot of laughter and mockery of Choctaw law and naïveté by the assembled white men, but their faces turned ashen an hour before dusk when a wagon driven by Simeon Silon arrived, carrying his wife and his coffin.

Not a man mocked Simeon Silon or Choctaw law after that. Hardy had felt a knot in his throat and never had he seen so many hardened men with moist eyes. Though he was not a tall man, Simeon Silon stood above every other man present when he reported to Choctaw police and asked them where he was to meet his executioner the next day at noon.

Then Simeon Silon drove his wagon fifty yards away from the impromptu camp of spectators. In the dwindling light of day he wrote out his last will and testament. The spectators in the adjoining camp were so hushed after dark that they could hear Simeon Silon enjoying his wife on the final night of his life.

While everyone else still seemed rattled the next morning, Simeon Silon had awakened and gone to the creek to bathe. He put on clean britches and a new white shirt and marched to his fate without a hitch in his stride, a quiver of his lip or a tremor of his muscle. It was a solemn spectacle, the only blot on the dignity of the ceremony being the photographer who set up his cumbersome camera to record the gruesome scene.

The Choctaw police sat him on a blanket that would become his death shroud and pulled his feet out in front of him, spreading his legs. Then they made Simeon Silon lean slightly back and rest on his outstretched arms as they unbuttoned his shirt and placed a spot of talcum powder on his chest over his heart.

At the appointed hour of noon, the head Choctaw lawman picked up the rifle and marched before Simeon Silon, who never blinked or said a thing. The lawman stood and aimed, but could not pull the trigger, the gun quivering in his hands so that even had he fired he might have missed completely.

"I cannot do it," the executioner had cried out, then handed the rifle to his top deputy. "I command you to carry out the judgment of the law and quickly."

The deputy received the rifle, and Simeon Silon sat as motionless as a statue. The deputy took quick aim and fired, a red splotch appearing on Simeon Silon's chest beside the dab of white powder. Silon fell backward, quivering and jerking, as his body tried to stave off death. In his haste, the deputy had missed Simeon Silon's heart.

"Shoot him again," spectators had shouted, but the Choctaw police were powerless to obey. The execution order had said he was to die by a single bullet, and that bullet had been fired. For thirty minutes the unconscious Silon writhed on the ground as the Choctaws debated the quandaries of Choctaw law. Then the policeman who could not pull the trigger to begin with jerked his kerchief from around his neck.

"I cannot let him suffer more," he cried and fell beside Silon, smothering him with the cloth.

Hardy had never seen a braver man than Simeon Silon nor a more merciful act than the Choctaw lawman with the kerchief. Hardy had walked away on wobbly knees and he had heard that some witnesses had disappeared into the forest to retch where no one would see them. Hardy never questioned the honor of the Choctaw people again. They had some bad apples, of course, but they were people of integrity, the kind of people that his own son could learn from. A year after the execution, Hardy had passed near the home of Simeon Silon. He had gathered a handful of wild flowers and placed them with a silver dollar upon the Choctaw's grave.

Silon's death seemed to jinx the Atoka place and the family that rushed in to claim it soon left, starting rumors that at night it was haunted by Silon's spirit or the ghosts of the seven Atokas. Hardy didn't truck to the idea of ghosts, figuring the most likely place within a thousand miles to be haunted was the gallows at Fort Smith. Hardy had passed by the gallows hundreds of times day and night and not once seen or heard any sign of a ghost.

Hardy whistled and the gray started down the hill that fell gently into the broad valley. Hardy was saddened by how far the Atoka place had fallen in three years, from model farm to run-down brothel. Hardy knew he must talk to Kitten, if she were indeed the madam. He had heard rumors before he retired that Bud frequented her. Hardy knew, though, he must be careful. Nothing created more excitement at a whorehouse than a man with a badge.

He approached the house unseen and tied his horse away from the trio that stood switching flies and stamping the ground out front. He walked quietly through the gateless opening in the waist-high picket fence, then spotted the gate where some rambunctious or dissatisfied customer had tossed it. The path to the front steps and porch was a wide rut from heavy use. Hardy's silent approach went unnoticed until he lifted his boot onto the porch step. The dry wood creaked and groaned. Every step across the wide porch heralded his arrival before he reached the door.

As he grabbed the doorknob, he heard a strident voice yelling from inside. "Another customer," called a worldly voice that had known too little love and too much lust.

Hardy twisted the handle and pushed the door open, stepping into the parlor to face a lethargic woman with stringy blond hair and her exposed legs stretched out on a worn sofa. She twisted strands of her hair around her finger. "You must be planning on making a day out of it, getting here this early," she said in that strident voice. "If you've got the money, I'm all the woman you'll need." She stood up, letting her gown fall open where he could glimpse her wares.

"I came for Kitten."

"She's in the . . . ," the blond stopped cold as her eyes came to rest on the badge. "Never heard of any Kitten." The hard woman turned suddenly modest, her fingers flying to button her gown.

Hardy closed the door with a little more authority than was necessary. "Where's Kitten?"

As he stepped toward her, she bolted for the hall-way. "The law's here," she screamed, "the law's here."

Cat quick, Hardy grabbed the woman's arm and jerked her to him. His grip tightened around her trembling flesh. "Where's Kitten?"

From several rooms came the commotion of women's screams, men's curses, squeaking bedsprings and scrambling footsteps as customers tried to gather their clothes and escape.

Doors flew open in the hallway and three men in varying states of dress bolted for the back door. Hardy pulled his pistol. "Stop, unless you want me to shoot."

The trio stopped and turned sheepishly around. One, wearing nothing but his boots, held the wad of clothes that was his shirt, pants and hat in front of his naked waist.

"Where's Kitten?" he demanded.

The men stood blank-faced before him.

Hardy nodded. "Any you boys married?" The question took the starch out of two of them. "Adultery's a crime I can arrest you for in Indian Territory, take you back to Fort Smith and put you on trial. I'd even invite your wives, think they would enjoy that?"

Both men paled, shaking their heads and biting their lips.

"I'm gonna ask one more time and if I don't get an answer, the correct answer, I'll take you in chains and your drawers back to Fort Smith."

The men looked at one another, shook their heads, then pointed to the first door in the hall. "That's her room," said the one with his clothes at his waist.

Hardy nodded. "You boys step outside, put your clothes on and don't let me see your ugly faces again, unless you want to appear before Judge Isaac Parker and explain where you've been dangling your dingers." Hardy waved the pistol toward the back door. Needing no more encouragement, they scrambled outside.

Releasing the blond, Hardy shoved his pistol back in his holster and advanced down the hall. He saw the heads of four women peeking out of hallway doors as he approached Kitten's room. He shoved the door open and walked inside. Kitten was an abundant woman with her ample bosom straining against the thin cotton cloth of her nightgown. She sat with her back against an iron bedstead and her knees bent as if she were reading something in her lap. Hardy saw nothing in her lap and noted her right hand was hidden under the bed sheet.

"My, my," answered the woman in a raspy, wheezing voice, "a gentleman with a badge. Didn't know there was such a thing. In fact, I bet you're the famed Doyle Hardy."

Hardy nodded.

"Well, sir, I'm glad to meet you. Just call me 'Kitten,' " she said, scooting her bare legs off the side of the bed and lifting her right arm still under the cover. "Let me shake your hand."

Beneath the sheet Hardy made out the straight line of a gun barrel in profile. He jumped aside, flinging his hat for the woman's painted eyes, just as she fired. The room exploded, the bullet thudding into the door behind Hardy, the sheet catching fire from the burned powder.

Hardy lunged for the bed as the woman tried to draw another bead on him, but the gun tangled in the sheet long enough for Hardy to grab her wrist, squeezing her hand until she screamed in pain. "Drop it," he demanded through clenched teeth.

She screamed as the gun fell from her hand onto the mattress. Hardy jerked her out of bed onto the floor, then threw back the sheet, grabbed the gun and threw it out the open window. Then he slapped at the flame licking at the edges of the bullet hole. He spat on the blackened spot to make sure the flame was out for good.

"Hell, deputy, why don't you just pull out your plumbing and piss on it while you're at it." Her gown bunched up around her waist, Kitten sat with her pudgy legs spread as she massaged her limp wrist. "Bud said you'd be here, knew you'd take out after him. I just didn't expect you so soon."

Hardy heard noises behind him and turned to see five women peeking into Kitten's room. "You ladies go about your business."

"Tarnation, deputy," said the blond who had greeted him at the door, "you scared away our business."

The other harlots laughed, the joke punctuated by the sound of three galloping horses outside.

"Scatter," Hardy ordered and all but the stringy-haired blond obeyed. She stared at Kitten a moment. Out of the corner of his eye, Hardy thought he saw Kitten give a slight nod.

Then the blond disappeared back down the hall and Hardy heard the back door swing open.

"Where's she going?" Hardy demanded.

"To feed our horses," Kitten answered.

Hardy knew he should stop the blond because no one fed horses in a nightgown unless there was a trick. However, he didn't plan on staying at the brothel much longer. He retrieved his hat. "Why'd you shoot?"

"Bud said he'd pay five hundred dollars to whoever killed you."

Hardy shook his head in disgust. "Bud doesn't have five hundred dollars."

Kitten shrugged. "But he does have a way with words and women."

Hardy scoffed. "Tell that to his wife who I buried yesterday."

"Less competition for me and my girls."

Fighting the urge to slap her, Hardy stepped to the window at the sound of another horse galloping away. He caught a glimpse of the blond astride an appaloosa. "Where's she going, to alert Bud?"

"Riding, you fool, she's going riding."

"Where's Bud hiding?"

Kitten laughed. "It ought to surprise you to know he ain't hiding. He said to tell you he was going to Boggy Depot and he was alerting the whole country-side you'd be following him. He figures there are a lot of men out there who'd gladly kill you for a lot less than the five hundred dollars he's offering." She laughed crazily, then started wheezing and gasping for breath. "Your boy thinks a lot of you," she managed.

Hardy turned and exited Kitten's room, slamming the door behind him. He glared down the hall and the remaining girls ducked back in their rooms like painted turtles hiding in their shells. He strode out the front door, taking wide steps across the creaking porch and bounding across the yard and through the opening in the picket fence to his horse. Untying the gray, he led the animal around the back to a watering trough, allowing the gelding to drink and blow for a moment. Then he mounted and headed down the road toward Boggy Depot.

He had ridden a couple of minutes when he heard galloping hooves as he approached the rise that carried him out of the small valley. His hand fell instinctively to his gun, then relaxed as an appaloosa with the stringy-haired blond topped the rise. Her hair fanned out behind her and her cotton blouse clung to her shapely bosom as she passed and shouted an obscenity at him. It made Hardy sick to his stomach that Bud had been hanging out with this type of women when he had a decent wife like Molina.

Atop the rise, the road narrowed then began to twist among the tall pines. He was still thinking about the sinister side of his son when he caught an unnatural movement at the side of the road among the trees. It was then he remembered Kirby Sands's warning about Flem Thurman, who lived near the brothel. That was who the blond had gone to warn.

Instinctively, Hardy ducked, just as a man in overalls pulled the twin triggers of a double-barreled shotgun. The piny trees reverberated with the blast and Hardy felt a burning pain in his shoulder and side.

The gray bolted down the road and Doyle Hardy rolled out of the saddle. He slammed to the ground, pain jolting through his left side and shoulder. He cursed at the agony shooting through his arm. Over the hoofbeats of his stampeding horse, he heard Flem Thurman's shout.

"Got you, you son of a bitch. Easiest five hundred dollars I ever made."

Still dazed from the fall, Hardy twisted his head in time to see Thurman break apart his double-barreled shotgun and shake loose the still smoking pair of hulls. Thurman shoved a fist inside a pocket of his overalls and pulled out two more shells.

Hardy knew he had to act quickly or the next barrage would kill him. He clambered to his hands and knees.

Flem Thurman's toothless smile became a gasp of surprise as Hardy's right hand slid for the .45-caliber Peacemaker at his side. Thurman shoved the shotgun shells for the open breech, but missed. He cursed.

Hardy rose on his knees, pulling the Colt from his holster.

His nerve escaping as fast as Hardy's gelding, Flem Thurman made another stab at loading his shotgun. One shell tumbled from his hand to the dirt.

Hardy lifted his pistol.

Despite his shaking fingers, Flem Thurman managed to shove the remaining shell into the barrel. The toothless smile reappeared on his face as he snapped the barrel shut with a sinister click and swung its gaping black eyes toward Hardy.

Thumbing back the hammer on his revolver, Hardy took aim where the gallus of Thurman's overalls snapped to the bib over his heart.

Flem Thurman pulled back the hammer on the shotgun.

Hardy squeezed the trigger and his Peacemaker bucked in his hand. By the red blossom on Thurman's chest and the bewildered look sliding across his face, Hardy knew his aim had been true. Flem Thurman took a step toward Hardy, then fell stiffly forward, like a downed tree. The jar of the fall detonated the shotgun, kicking up a cloud of road dust that mingled with the smell of burned gunpowder.

Beyond Thurman, Hardy heard the sound of galloping hooves gradually slowing as the stringy-haired harlot brought her appaloosa to a halt atop the gentle hill Hardy had descended before the assassination attempt. Slowly, Hardy stood up, then swung his pistol around toward her, squeezing off a shot to scare her back to the brothel. She jerked the horse around by the reins and disappeared at a gallop over the hill.

Hardy didn't care for her or anyone else to know

he had been wounded. The pain came in waves. After sliding his pistol back in his holster, he glanced at his shoulder. There were a dozen or more tiny holes in the broadcloth coat. Hardy figured he had been hit by the perimeter of the shot pattern. Had he not ducked, the shotgun blast likely would have blown his head off.

Hardy managed to walk over to Thurman's body and jerk the shotgun from beneath him. Easing to the closest pine tree, Hardy drew back the shotgun in his right hand and began to beat it against the tree trunk. Through the trees, he saw the primitive log cabin that had been Thurman's home and a mule hitched out front. Tossing the broken shotgun aside, he staggered toward the mule, then remembered Marshal Yoes's rule prohibiting the use of a prisoner's property for any reason.

The realization that Thurman was not his prisoner, never had been, brought a smile to Hardy's face as he staggered the rest of the way to the mule. The saddled mule stood switching flies. As Hardy approached, the mule turned its head and stared at him with mournful eyes. Catching the slight scent of Hardy's blood, the mule stamped nervously until Hardy stroked the brown fur on his neck.

"Easy, boy," he said as he untied the mule and struggled his way aboard the animal. The mule reacted to the slightest movement of the reins. Hardy gave a hollow laugh. Whatever Flem Thurman lacked as a shotgun marksman, he more than made up for as a trainer of mules. Hardy guided the mule wide of Thurman's body so the animal would not catch the aroma of his blood. He emerged back on the trail about a half mile down from where Flem Thurman was sprawled beside the road. Hardy would let someone else do the burying because he had his gray gelding to find and then his son.

A mile beyond where Hardy had emerged from the trees, he found his gray, gently grazing in a meadow of tall grass and spring flowers. The gray lifted its head a moment to stare at the approaching animal and rider, then resumed its peaceful grazing.

Hardy rode up beside the gelding and reached down for the reins. He dismounted from the mule, then slapped it across the neck. "Shoo," he shouted and the mule jumped away from him, kicking his hind legs at the air before breaking into a trot for Thurman's place. Hardy wondered how many of Yoes's rules he had just broken.

Feeling faint for a moment, Hardy grabbed the saddle horn and leaned his head against the saddle leather. He caught his breath and tried to shake his left arm of the pain and his mind of the muddle the wound had induced.

He gathered enough of his strength to crawl atop the saddle and start the gelding back down the road toward Boggy Depot. Hardy rode slumped in the saddle, the gelding finding is own pace and its own way. Hardy gritted his teeth against the pain, staring through squinted eyes down the road. At times he sensed himself swaying in the saddle as if he were about to fall, but from somewhere he found the strength to keep his balance. Sometimes he seemed to black out for an instant, then come to with a start. He shook his head to help stay as alert as possible, but that only started the pain to coursing through his left side again. He lost track of time, not knowing how far he had come nor where the gray was taking him. Once when he found the energy to lift his head and judge the sky, he realized the day was already past high sun. All he understood for certain was the thirst clawing at his throat and the hunger grabbing at his belly.

Finally, he felt the horse stop and he tried to focus his blurry eyes. Before him—if he wasn't hallucinating—was a modest stone house and two wide-eyed kids staring at him. He tried to say something, but his dry throat had robbed him of his voice, and when he attempted to dismount, his foot slipped from the stirrup and he slid to the ground, just managing to avoid a total collapse by grabbing the saddle horn with his right hand. From somewhere far away, he heard the excited call of two children. "Big Ma, Big Ma," they yelled, "come quick! This man is hurt."

Hardy blacked out until he felt moisture upon his lips. With his stiff tongue he licked at the wetness and felt a trickle of water slide down his throat. Batting his eyelids, he strained to focus upon this quivering apparition that swayed above him. The sunlight was so bright overhead, that he had to squint to see and when he finally made out the form of a woman's face, it seemed swathed in a halo of golden light. Hardy had never been one to believe in angels, but the visage changed his mind. For a moment he did not know if he were dead and heaven was a sip of water or if this was some earthly benefactor. He had seen the painted representations of angels that the stationers sold in Fort Smith shops, but they were all young with fair skin, blue eyes and curly locks of blond hair. This angel, though, had straight black hair, dark eyes and lightly bronzed skin. She was not young, but neither was she old.

She squeezed the cloth at his mouth and water trickled between his lips and down his cheek. Hardy lapped at it greedily until she pulled the cloth away.

"More," he begged, his voice dry and raspy.

The angel leaned toward him and spoke softly. "You are too heavy for me and the little ones to carry inside. Do the best you can to stand and walk, then you shall have all the water you want."

The promise of water spurred Hardy to draw upon his last reserve of strength as he tried to sit up. The angel's firm hands tugged him under the shoulders. Hardy cried out at her touch, then thought of water and gritted his teeth against the agony.

His head fluttered with dizziness as he managed an upright position, but she would not allow him to rest, forcing him to struggle to his feet. He stood for a moment on wobbly knees, then felt her slide under his right arm and slip her arm around his waist. She started him toward the house and Hardy felt a pair of tiny arms slip around his left legs in a puny effort to help.

Hardy closed his eyes and moved where he was steered. For several steps he advanced in the sun's warm glare, then the light was muted as he stepped into the shade of the house. His feet moved tentatively on the hardwood floor as he was steered through the furniture. After what seemed like a mile of walking, the angel eased him about and let him slide slowly back to a bed. She disappeared for a moment, then returned, lifting his head. Hardy detected the sweet smell of water and parted his dry lips. He felt a tin cup at his mouth and relished the water that she poured down his throat.

After drinking as much as she would give him, he collapsed on the bed and felt the angel removing his clothes. Her hands were gentle and the sheets were cool and those were the last things Hardy remembered before drifting off to sleep.

Hardy did not know how long he dozed, but he awoke to a tugging on his arm. He tried to move, but could not. As he opened his eyes, he saw a woman tying a leather thong around the bedpost. Then Hardy realized his right hand was tied to that thong. What was she doing? He tried to move his sore left hand, but it was immobilized as well, then he kicked his feet and they were tied as well. He lay naked and helpless on his stomach. She picked up an awl and a man's razor, then held them both over the flame of a candle she had stood in a pie tin at his side.

As she looked from the flame to his left shoulder, she realized he was staring at her. She smiled, then picked up a wet cloth with her free hand and moved it to his mouth. "I've got to get the shot out. I count thirteen wounds. Put the cloth between your teeth."

Nodding, Hardy opened his mouth and closed his eyes. When she placed the cloth in his mouth, he gritted his teeth around it, enjoying the moisture, then flinching at the pain as she began to explore each wound for the shot. Sometimes she dug into his flesh with the awl, other times she pressed his flesh between her thumb as she tried to work the tiny shot out. Every time she extracted a tiny ball of lead, she would drop it in the pie plate. Hardy counted the tings as the lead hit the tin, but after the sixth one he passed out from the pain.

Hardy remembered nothing except waking up

with a start. It was night and the very earth seemed to rumble. Then, through the window, he saw a flash of lightning that illuminated the countryside so brilliantly that Hardy could see the nearby barn as if it were daylight. The thunder broke immediately in the wake of the lightning and Hardy flinched from the reverberations which rattled the windows and made the whole house shake. Hardy twisted in bed, groaning at the dull ache in his left side, but realizing he was no longer bound.

In the next flash of lightning, he realized he was not alone. His doctoring angel sat in a rocking chair, staring at him.

Hardy remembered his gray and realized he must get the horse out of the weather. "My horse," he said, "my horse."

"The little ones put your horse in the barn. Your carbine and saddlebags are by the bed."

Letting out a long breath in relief, Hardy settled back into the comfortable mattress, just as another flash of lightning and clap of thunder preceded sheets of rain. "Thank you," he said softly.

"No," she answered, "it is I who should thank you."

Hardy did not understand. "What?"

"I should thank you. You are Doyle Hardy, the deputy marshal, are you not?"

He took his time answering, not knowing for sure if he should admit to his identity. But how could he not level with the woman who had helped him and sheltered his horse from the pelting rain outside? "I am."

"I'm Emma Sims. You may not remember me, but a dozen years ago, my two boys were turning bad, running with the whiskey peddlers, and getting into the mischief that would one day have brought them before Judge Parker himself."

Over the years Hardy had had so many encounters with whiskey peddlers that he did not remember this one for certain.

"You caught them, but you didn't chain them up and take them to Fort Smith. You gave them a second chance, brought them here to me and my husband."

The vague memory returned and Hardy seemed to recall beating the two boys with his fists when his lecture didn't work. Hardy bit his lips. "These aren't the same two I whipped, are they?"

"It's them," she said. "They would not listen to right and wrong from their father. They were cocky, like boys of fifteen and sixteen, figuring they could whip the world. You showed them otherwise and promised them you'd be back to give them more if they didn't behave like their mother and father told them. You humbled their wild side and saved their lives. They are a joy to my soul, now that my man died, near on two years ago. They have fine wives and families and live not five miles away. The little ones who first saw you are theirs, my grandchildren."

Hardy sighed. Why hadn't he ever done what it took to keep Bud Hardy from taking up his evil life?

"I prayed that one day I might be able to thank you for what you did. Now I have that chance and it is a good thing since you have a heart as heavy as the rains outside."

"What do you mean?"

"I know of your son and the terrible crime he committed against his family and I know some men are looking to kill you. The rain is good because it will wash away your trail so no one can follow you here. It will give you a few days to recover from your wounds. But now you must rest."

She stood up from her rocking chair and retreated to another room. Hardy fell asleep to the patter of the dwindling rain as the storm moved on.

8

Doyle Hardy awoke to the sound of giggling. Opening his eyes, he saw the two little ones grinning at him and nudging one another. Barely six years old, the two boys had thick manes of black hair, wide dark eyes and smiles that matched the midmorning sunshine streaming in through the open window.

At the sight of his open eyes, they raced to the window. "Big Ma, Big Ma," they yelled, "he's awake."

In a minute, Hardy saw Emma Sims pass by the window, carrying a hoe in one hand and a basket of eggs in the other. She wore a bonnet and a bright calico dress that seemed too new to be worn for chores.

He started to throw off the sheets, but realized he had nothing on. He grimaced at the dull aching throb in his shoulder, but admitted it wasn't nearly as bad as it had been the day before, thanks to Emma's surgery and the bandage tightly wrapped around his chest and shoulder.

The taller of the two boys picked up a pie tin from the floor and eased bashfully toward the bed.

Now that Hardy was fully awake, the two boys seemed less courageous. The boy held the tin where Hardy could see the lead shot extracted from his shoulder and side.

"Did these hurt?"

Hardy nodded. "Like fire."

"Why were you shot?"

"Some men don't want to live by the law."

The smaller of the two boys edged up to the bed. "Did you kill the man that did this?"

Reluctantly Hardy nodded.

Mouths agape, the two boys looked at one another wide-eyed.

"What did he say when you killed him?" the taller asked, just as his grandmother entered the room.

Emma clucked her tongue and flushed the boys away. "Little ones, that is the business of the law, not yours."

"Yes, Big Ma," they replied.

"And," she waved her finger at their noses, "you are to tell no one that Deputy Hardy is with us. Some men want to do him harm and he needs time to recover. If anyone comes to the house, you say you have seen no one."

"Yes, Big Ma," they answered before escaping out the door.

Emma Sims turned to Hardy, grabbed the pie tin and put it on the washstand at the end of the bed. "The little ones had no need to show you that." Removing her bonnet, she smiled. "How do you feel?"

"Weak, a bit stiff and plenty sore, but better."

"You lost much blood. I'm soaking your clothes. I will wash them this afternoon. Maybe you can wear what my sons left of my husband's things."

"What happened to your husband?"

There was a pause in her smile. "Two years ago June, I found him dead in the garden. He just died on me, a peaceful death like his life. He was a good man, an honest man, who never beat me or my sons. He died doing honest work. We buried him on the place where he could watch over me."

"I'm sorry."

"It's been hard, but I get by. My sons help as best they can, but they've got families of their own to support and places of their own to work. They let the boys keep me company and help with the chores, but it's not the same as having a man about."

For some reason, she seemed suddenly embarrassed and turned her eyes from him. Hardy did not understand until she spoke.

"Please do not think me a bad woman for undressing you entirely. I meant by having a man about, someone to talk to and cook for."

Hardy held up his right hand and shook his head. "I have nothing but respect and gratitude for you."

She smiled again. "Are you hungry?"

"Very."

"I've gathered eggs and I've plenty of salt pork. I can make a batch of sourdough biscuits and coffee."

"Sounds good. If you could just have one of the boys help me with my saddlebags, I've got an extra pair of long johns I could wear under your husband's clothes."

Emma called for the boys and they ran into the room. "Get his saddlebags," she instructed as she moved toward the kitchen. The two raced to the bed and lifted the saddlebags, just managing to shove them onto the sheet covering Hardy.

"Why is it so heavy?" the taller one asked.

"Extra ammunition," Hardy answered as he unbuckled a leather strap and threw open the flap on one of the compartments.

"You must know many bad men," said the shorter one.

Both boys pointed and giggled when Hardy pulled out the clean, white, cotton long johns. "You boys better leave or I'll make you wear clothes like these."

The boys made faces at one another, then darted out the door.

Hardy pulled the long johns beneath the sheet and squirmed into them. Without too much pain he managed to work them over his legs and to his waist, then he slid his good right arm through the sleeve, pulling up the top as he did. He tried to guide his sore left arm inside, but he quickly tired of fighting the pain. Instead, he pulled the top of the union suit over his shoulder and let the left sleeve fall limply to his side. He buttoned the underwear up to his chest, then caught his breath. He was tired still.

From the kitchen wafted the aroma of fresh coffee, frying salt pork and baking biscuits. Emma Sims waltzed in a few minutes later and dug through a drawer in her bureau, pulling out a pair of wool socks, a pair of worn corduroy pants and a baggy pullover shirt. She tossed them on the bed. "These aren't as fancy as yours and probably are a mite small."

"They're cleaner than mine."

"Yours will be clean once I get through with the washing," she said as she retreated to the kitchen.

The floor was cool to the touch of his bare feet as he slid from under the sheet and sat up. For the first time he realized how truly weak he was. It took his full energy to fight the dizziness and maintain his balance. When his head cleared as much as he thought it would, he reached for the pants and slid them over his calves, then up his thighs as high as he could. He took a deep breath, then eased away from the mattress, wobbling precariously while trying to overcome the wave of dizziness that swirled in his head. He closed his eyes and grabbed the britches, pulling them to his waist. Though the pants were tight, he was able to button them. Sitting back on the bed, he took the socks and put them on. Only then did he realize the trousers were a good six inches short of his ankle. He reached for the shirt, then decided against expending the effort. Hardy leaned back on the pillow, breathing heavily from the exertion. As much as he hated to admit it, it would be a few days before he was fit enough to resume the hunt for Bud Hardy.

He dozed off until he felt Emma Sims's hand upon his arm. "Food's ready." She eased him to a sitting position, then helped him stand, giving him plenty of time to find his balance before assisting him to the kitchen table.

Hardy saw the little ones pointing and giggling at his attire and he realized how silly and helpless he must look. He couldn't help but smile.

"Hush," Emma chided them.

"Yes, Big Ma," they answered as their grandmother steered Hardy into a chair and eased it up to the table.

She hovered over him, scooping a generous helping of scrambled eggs from a bowl onto his plate, then placing a half dozen slices of bacon beside them. She plucked a trio of hot biscuits from a pan just out of the oven and buttered them for him.

"Smells good," Hardy said, picking up a fork and stabbing at the eggs. He didn't know if he had the energy to lift the fork to his face. His hand quivered. Emma, though, wrapped her fingers around his and guided the food to his mouth. Eggs never tasted better. His body seemed to perk up at each bite and he let his hand fall to his plate for more. Emma guided his hand for several bites of egg, bacon and biscuit. The food seemed to restore much of his missing strength and gradually to eliminate his dizziness. When Emma released her hold, he attacked the rest of the food voraciously, eating heartily of second and third helpings and consuming the entire pan of biscuits.

Once he looked up and saw Emma smiling at his appetite. Her smile was as invigorating as the food. After years of living with the cold Tinnie, it was satisfying to see a woman take pleasure at his appetite.

When he had cleared his plate, he took his coffee cup and settled back in his chair, drawing deeply on the aromatic liquid. He felt a smile work its way across his face as he looked at Emma. "The meal fit me just fine, even if the clothes don't."

Emma snickered. Her laugh had the ring of sincerity, like the happy toll of Christmas bells in Fort Smith. How long had it been since he had enjoyed a woman's laugh?

"You will have your old clothes back by nightfall, washed, dried and ironed," she answered, as if the work would be pleasure rather than another chore.

Hardy studied her closely and the longer he looked at her, the more he appreciated her subtle beauty. It was not the beauty of a young girl, but of a mature woman his own age, one whose inner beauty over the years had exceeded her physical charms. Even so, the fullness to her figure, the sparkle in her black eyes, the cut of her dark hair and the curve of her lips could rekindle the urges of any decent man.

The light bronze of her skin suggested there had been more than Choctaw among her ancestors. He found himself wanting her in ways a married man shouldn't consider. She seemed to realize his thoughts and lowered her head shyly.

"I did not mean to stare," he apologized.

"I don't mind," she said softly. "I am a widow."

As she began to clear the table, Hardy managed to stand up by himself. With food in his stomach, his dizziness abated and he seemed more certain of himself as he eased back to the bedroom.

He had no sooner plopped on the bed than Emma was beside him, helping him lift his feet, then pulling off the ill-fitting pants. "You rest," she said as she drew the sheet over him. "Bad men may be looking for you. Some say your son has put five hundred dollars on your head like a common murderer. If strangers ride up, I will have the little ones warn you. Your gun belt and carbine are beneath the bed." She picked up his saddlebags from the mattress and slid them under the bed as well.

"Thank you for your hospitality," Hardy answered.

She moved to the window, opening it wider to invite more of the breeze inside. "Could I ask one thing of you, Doyle Hardy?"

Hardy twisted around to look at her, wondering what favor she might possibly ask. It would disappoint him if she asked for money, though she well deserved it. "Yes, I'm indebted to you."

"No," she replied, "I am still indebted to you for saving my sons. When the little ones go home tomorrow, I should like to have them tell my sons, their fathers, to come and meet you again."

Hardy was angered at himself for thinking she might ask for money. "I'd be honored to visit with them. It's always a pleasure to meet with the decent folks of Choctaw Nation."

Emma smiled and departed without another word.

For the rest of the day, Hardy fell in and out of sleep. The boys brought him occasional glasses of water and checked on him while their grandmother worked. At one point, he heard her ordering her grandsons to help build a fire for the wash pot and another time instructing them to go milk the cow. About dusk he awoke to find Emma placing his clothes upon the chair. His boiled shirt, pressed pants and suit coat seemed like new except for the tiny holes where the buckshot had hit. Atop his shirt, she had placed his tie, the warrant for Bud Hardy and the pamphlet of Marshal Yoes's rules. Beside the shirt she had placed his long johns, washed and folded, but stained where the blood from his wounds had been absorbed. When he smelled the aroma of supper cooking, Hardy found the strength to get out of bed and put on his pants. With effort, he managed to get his left arm into the sleeve of his long johns. Next he pulled on the clean shirt, not bothering to tuck it into his pants.

When he entered the kitchen, Emma turned from over the hot stove and smiled. "Your color has come back."

"It's the clean clothes," he answered and she seemed pleased.

"Supper will be done shortly. I hope you like fried chicken."

"Very much, it's my favorite."

Until Emma covered the table with food, he did not realize how busy she had been all day. Besides the fried chicken, she set out bowls of boiled yams, fried onions, creamed gravy, fresh corn bread, red beans, chowchow and a stack cake for dessert.

When the little ones joined them at the table, Emma gave the boys a drumstick and a thigh each, then served Hardy both breasts and the wish bone. He protested that he was getting too much and tried to put a breast on her plate, but she would have none of that, taking for herself the backbone which was skimpy on meat.

Hardy filled his plate generously and ate robustly, enjoying every bite. His stomach seemed as big as a canyon and he tried to fill every bit of it, again taking seconds and thirds of everything. On top of that, he had three slices of stack cake for dessert.

When he polished off the last of his meal, he knew one thing for certain—Emma's fried chicken was damn sure better than Tinnie's.

9

Despite his injuries, the next two days were about as pleasant as Doyle Hardy could remember in years. Emma Sims tended him and cooked tasty meals. On the next evening after she had sent the little ones back home on their horses, she pulled two rocking chairs out on the narrow porch and asked Hardy to join her. They talked about the news of Choctaw Nation while she sat with her sewing basket at her side and his coat in her lap, trying to stitch up the holes in his coat.

Her hand brushed against papers in an inside pocket and she pulled them out, embarrassing herself when she realized she held the warrant for Hardy's son.

"It is a terrible thing," she apologized. "I know because I feared my sons would bring shame to my husband's name and mine."

The subject was one Hardy cared to discuss with no one, yet he seemed oddly at ease with her mention of Bud. Still, he did not know what to say.

"It seems unfair," Emma said after a pause, "that you should save my two sons but lose your one."

Hardy shook his head. "I failed him."

"No, we fail because of ourselves, not because of our parents."

After years with Tinnie, Hardy had forgotten how softly and wisely a woman could speak. And sometimes, as now, how a silence between a man and a woman could say more than mere words. Maybe it was just the thought of being valued by a woman that made the silence so satisfying. Living day after day with Tinnie, Hardy knew the gall of a hateful silence, but this was a peaceful, inviting quiet.

They sat quietly, the only noise was the rocking of their chairs and the sounds of birds singing in the trees. A couple of hours after dark, they moved inside, Hardy sufficiently strong to carry the rocking chairs into the house. Hardy went to his bed and she to hers. Though his shoulder pained him less, sleep came sporadically.

Come morning he heard her in the kitchen early, making breakfast. He was dressed by the time she announced breakfast. He startled her by his immediate entrance and she dropped a pot onto the cookstove.

It was a big soup pot. "I don't know what you're cooking, but I don't think I can eat that much."

She smiled. "My sons will be here by noon today. We'll have plenty of stew to feed them."

Hardy took his seat, helping himself to eggs, bacon and biscuits. After breakfast, he made a quick trip to the barn to check on his gray gelding, which he found well fed and watered, though anxious to run, and then rushed back inside the house. He wanted to stay out of sight as much as possible so no harm might visit Emma during his stay.

Half an hour before noon, Hardy was relaxing on

his bed when he heard the noise of an approaching wagon and horses. He jumped up and grabbed his pistol from beneath the bed, then eased to the front room and peeked out the window. Three horsemen accompanied a farm wagon which trailed another saddled mount. Two of the horsemen, though, were not men at all but boys. The little ones had returned with their fathers.

Hardy lowered his pistol and hoped to slip back into his bedroom before Emma saw his weapon. He was surprised to see her standing in the door. He grimaced. "It's your sons and grandsons."

"It is good that you are careful. It sounds like Newt is returning his father's wagon. I hope you like my sons. They have become good, dependable men who will help look after their mother in her old age."

"You're too good-looking a woman to think yourself old," he said as he returned his gun to the holster beneath his bed.

"I'm forty-eight," she said, as if fishing for his reaction.

"That's two years younger than me, and I ain't old. A bit run down, maybe, but not old."

Emma giggled, then pointed out the window as the wagon passed the house. "My sons will tend the horses and unhook the wagon first."

"I'd help," Hardy offered, "but I figure I need to keep out of sight."

"Don't worry, the little ones will be here as soon as they dismount."

Emma retreated to the kitchen and Hardy stepped to the window, watching the two men and the two boys approach the barn. The two boys jumped from their saddles, tied their reins around a hitching ring and bolted for the house, racing each other to the back door. With a clatter of stampeding feet on the plank floor, they entered the kitchen.

"What are we eating, Big Ma?" asked the taller boy.

"Did you make sweets?" asked the other.

Emma laughed as Hardy entered.

"Hello, deputy," the shorter one said.

"Stew with corn bread and fried apple pies," Emma announced.

The boys burst out of the kitchen and ran to their fathers, proclaiming the noon menu. After five minutes, the boys returned, followed shortly by their fathers.

As they entered the kitchen, both men removed their hats and stood awkwardly with them before their waists, a bit shy and uncertain what their mother wanted of them.

"Sons, you remember Doyle Hardy?"

They both nodded slightly, a bit embarrassed.

"I wanted him to see what fine men you became."

Hardy extended his hand and stepped toward them. They were lean, good-looking men with bronzed skin, sharp eyes like their mother and hair cut shorter than was common in The Nations. They wore gun belts, though their pistols rode high on their hips, not low as was the fashion for many bad men. Hardy grabbed the hand of the first one and shook it warmly.

"That's Newt," Emma announced. "He's my oldest."

Moving to the next man, Hardy grabbed his hand as well. "And that is Tate."

"Glad to meet both of you. Your momma's been real helpful to me the last few days. Her and the little ones."

Both men smiled.

"They make more noise than a band of Indians," Tate joked.

"We are Indians, Pa, Choctaw," the tall one answered, missing the humor.

Emma herded the men and boys to the table, then began to ladle steaming hot stew into bowls and place them in front of each guest. Grabbing their spoons, the two boys began to blow on the soup.

"Wait until Big Ma joins us," commanded Newt.

Emma set a pan of corn-bread muffins on the table, then nodded to the boys. They attacked the stew with relish.

Hardy thought Emma's sons were made uncomfortable by his presence, since it brought back bad memories from their wilder youth, but he didn't know quite how to change that.

Finally, Newt spoke up. "You aren't the devil I remember, Deputy Hardy. I thought you were eight feet tall with fists of stone the way you whipped us."

"Yeah," Tate added, "I always wondered why you didn't take us to jail like the rest."

It was a question for which Hardy had no certain answer. "Maybe I saw a decent streak in you I didn't see in the others. Maybe I knew I'd need your mother to nurse me back to health in a few years."

"I never took a drink of liquor since that day," Tate said.

"Yeah," Newt broke in, "I guess if we'd kept up the drinking and troublemaking we could've wound up like Simeon Silon, murdering that poor Atoka family."

"I guess we owe you our thanks," Tate said, "though I would've never thought so at the time as bruised and hurt as I was. I'd seen a lot of fights, but I never saw anyone come near being the rabid cougar you were that day."

Hardy nodded. "Thanks enough is seeing you've grown into two dependable men, farmers I guess?"

"Yes, sir," said Newt. "We try our hand at that, run a little livestock, chop wood for folks, set fence posts, whatever we can to earn a few dollars."

Hardy glanced at Emma and saw her beaming with delight that her sons now conversed freely with him. Emma made herself busy, refilling bowls and pulling another pan of corn-bread muffins out of the oven. Then she served the fried pies. The kids ate a pie apiece and grabbed another to take outside while they played. Once they left the kitchen, their fathers glanced at one another, Tate motioning for Newt to speak.

"Deputy Hardy," Newt started, "we was wondering if we might get you to do a favor for us." He seemed embarrassed to have to ask, the Choctaws having an independent streak in them.

When Newt's courage seemed to lag, Tate spoke up. "We don't want our boys facing some of the same temptations we did. And, you see, there's this still that's been operating a couple miles from our place by a white man and a black man. Bad men, both. Could you maybe arrest them, get them away from us?"

Hardy was touched that they had asked this as a favor. Maybe the whipping had done more good than he would ever have imagined. "Be glad to. That's what riding Choctaw Nation is all about."

The two brothers smiled their appreciation and Hardy saw Emma's eyes glisten over with tears.

"The still's a mile off the Boggy Depot Road, between Willow Creek and Signal Hill."

Hardy nodded. He knew the general location. "I'll see if I can catch them, convince them that they don't linger in these parts any more." Hardy took a second pie when the little ones rushed into the house.

"Riders coming," said the tall one.

"Three," said the other.

Hardy threw down the pie and bolted to the bedroom. He feared it was the LeHew brothers. He jerked his holster from under the bed and buckled it around his waist. Then he pulled out his carbine and checked the load.

"What do we do?" Emma said.

Hardy motioned for her and her two sons to step out front. "Tell them you ain't seen me. I don't want any trouble here on your place because that'll just bring more problems for you and the little ones. If it looks like they're gonna pull a weapon on you, fall to the ground and I'll pick off as many as I can."

Then Hardy turned to Newt and Tate. "Go outside with your mother. Don't block my view through the window and whatever you do, don't let your hands fall near your pistols unless they pull guns."

Hardy crouched low and eased into the parlor, taking a position beside the window as the three men drew up ten yards from the front door.

"Hello, the house," called the one in the middle.

They were a sordid trio, the look of evil evident in their narrow eyes, unshaven cheeks and thin, snake-like lips. Upon seeing them, Hardy recognized the LeHew brothers.

"Hello, the house," repeated the one in the middle.

Emma moved toward the door, her sons following her.

"Afternoon," she called as she stepped outside, her two sons in her wake.

The one in the middle took off his hat. "Well, howdy, Injun friends," he said, his voice dripping with mockery, "I'm Satch LeHew and these here are my brothers, Jesse and Clyde LeHew. We've been looking for a friend that was seen in these parts a few days ago, Doyle Hardy, a deputy marshal. You folks ain't seen him have you?"

Emma shrugged. "We've no cause for the law to come looking for us."

"Damn upstanding Injun family, are you?" Satch LeHew answered. "Well, our friend the marshal, got himself shot in a whorehouse down the road Skullyville way, some type of dispute over a whore."

Hardy fought off a surge of anger at the lie and the impulse to barge out the door and challenge them. Through the screen of the lace curtain, Hardy studied the trio closely for any gesture that might forewarn of an attack on Emma or her sons.

Satch LeHew spat a murky stream of tobacco juice toward the porch. "Yeah, as we hear the story, he was a bedding some prostitute when the girl's pa found her. The old man tried to protect his daughter's virtue—she was a virgin I hear—and damned if our friend Deputy Hardy just didn't up and shoot him, but not before the old man fired off his scattergun."

"Yeah," interjected Jesse LeHew, "it was sort of a shotgun bedding." Jesse laughed at his own joke, but neither of his brothers appeared to understand.

"Shut up, Jesse," ordered Satch LeHew, who shook his hat and offered his biggest smile as he leaned forward in the saddle. "We know he done wrong, but he's hurt and we just want to help him before some folks find him and lynch him. He's an old coot, ain't got many years left. You seen anybody like that, Injun friends?"

Emma stepped toward Satch LeHew. "Nobody like that I've seen today."

"What about yesterday or the day before, old squaw?" Satch LeHew asked.

"No," said Emma, crossing her arms over her breast then turning to her boys. "Have you seen anything?"

They both shrugged.

"You're welcome to look about the place," Emma suggested, "just watch out for my grandsons. This man doesn't sound the kind I would want around them."

Satch LeHew nodded. "He's lower than a snake's belly."

Emma shook her head. "I would ask you in for a meal, but we finished all the stew. If you will stay here, I will go to the kitchen, fetch some corn bread and fried pies you can eat on the trail while you look for this man."

"Why that's mighty neighborly of you, squaw friend."

Emma turned around and marched into the house, never giving a glance in Hardy's direction as she continued her decoy.

Next Hardy heard Newt's voice. "This lawman you are looking for, is he the one with the five hundred dollars placed on his head by his son?"

Hardy watched Satch frown. "That's what we hear, Injun friend. We just want to find our pal before somebody hurts him. We'd sure appreciate it if you saw him to let us know. We're just trying to return a favor for an old pal, Injun friend. But if you try to take him, he's a mean cuss and just might kill you."

"Maybe five hundred dollars is worth the risk," answered Newt.

Behind him Hardy heard Emma emerging from the kitchen. She passed him and stepped outside, just as Tate was speaking.

"We could hunt and kill this man ourselves for five hundred dollars."

"Hush, my sons," scolded Emma. "I forbid you to hunt this man. Nothing good can come of it. We cannot get trapped in the white man's law."

Satch LeHew grinned. "That's what they need to hear, squaw friend."

Emma stepped off the porch, her extended arm offering the LeHew brothers a white dish towel, bloated at the bottom and tied at the top like a tobacco pouch. "Plenty of corn-bread muffins and fried pies to fight your hunger when you hunt this man."

Satch leaned forward in the saddle and grabbed the bag of food. "Obliged, squaw friend."

Emma waved her wrists at them. "Now go on, please, before you give my sons ideas that can get them killed or in trouble."

"Good enough, squaw friend, we'd hate to see either of your boys hurt, so you keep them working the farm here and out of our way." Satch tossed the bag of victuals to Clyde, then jerked the reins on his horse. The claybank gelding spun around and trotted off. Jesse and Clyde looked at one another, then jerked their bays around and followed.

Hardy sighed with relief and studied the LeHews' mounts, noting the yellowish hue of the claybank and the markings of the bays. Remembering the markings and color of their horses might buy him a few extra seconds of time should he encounter them somewhere down the trail. Though he lowered his carbine as Emma and her sons marched back inside, he kept his eyes focused toward the road until the three men aimed their horses toward Boggy Depot and disappeared in the trees.

When he turned to Emma, he saw a tremor in her hand.

"You did good," Hardy reassured her.

Newt stepped up to Hardy and clasped his hand

on his shoulder. "We didn't mean nothing by the reward money, just thought it might throw them off the trail."

Hardy nodded. "We must all live by our wits. I'd say yours and your mom's are pretty sharp."

Newt and his brother smiled.

"That is high praise from a man of your reputation," Tate said, reaching out and shaking Hardy's hand. "Now Newt and I must leave and return to our wives and our other children. We do not feel safe with those three so near. We will leave the little ones with Big Ma to protect her."

Hardy nodded. "I'll be leaving come morning, before I trouble you more."

"No trouble," Emma said, stepping to Hardy. "I hoped you would stay until you were stronger."

Hardy thought he detected disappointment in her voice.

10

Morning came too soon for Doyle Hardy. Though his arm was still sore and he had not regained all his strength, he feared his continued presence might bring harm to Emma Sims and her grandsons. He awoke an hour before dawn, planning to saddle his horse and leave without a good-bye. He did not want to appear ungrateful, but he figured a farewell would be harder than he cared to admit. Even as his feet touched the cold floor, he heard the sounds of movement from Emma's room and then from the kitchen.

As he was pulling on his striped pants, he saw the kitchen door come aglow with the light of a lamp. Then Emma stood before him, shyly pulling her gingham robe shut at the bosom.

"You don't need to fix breakfast," he said finding his shirt in the soft light seeping in from the kitchen, "you've done enough."

"I was awake and couldn't get back to sleep."

"Worried about the LeHew brothers?"

She bit her lip and shook her head. "Worried about you."

Hardy didn't know what to say. He was a married man, but her concern seemed so sincere. He could not remember the last time Tinnie had voiced a worry about him. Even when he went to town, she seldom asked where he was going and always acted like she didn't care if he returned. He knew if he gave in to the powerful emotions tugging at him that he would not get away before dawn and he had to be away before good light so no one would know that Emma had harbored him for four nights. "I must be gone by daybreak." Grabbing the shirt she had cleaned and patched, he pulled it on.

"I understand," she said, "but please eat breakfast with me."

She stood in the doorway until he nodded. "Thank you, Doyle Hardy."

He heard her turn around and retreat into the kitchen to begin breakfast. Hardy tucked in his shirt, then pulled his suspenders over his shoulders. He sat on the bed and started tugging on the socks she had loaned him, then paused. Hardy knew he should get his own socks, but he told himself they were too much trouble to find in his saddlebags, knowing all the time he was only using that as an excuse to keep something that reminded him of her. He tugged on his boots, then bent over and pulled his saddlebags out from under the bed, finding his extra pair of long johns and his socks neatly folded atop the leather. Opening the flap, he shoved his socks between two boxes of ammunition, then stuffed the underwear atop everything else.

The aroma of brewing coffee tickled his nose as he pulled his holster and revolver from under the tall bed. He buckled the gun belt around his waist, then retrieved his carbine and scabbard from the floor, tossing the weapon on the bed. By the chair where Emma had draped it all ironed and mended, he lifted his broadcloth coat and slipped it over his arms. The dull ache in his left shoulder was tolerable, even as he picked up his thin tie and knotted it around his collar. After placing his hat atop his head, sliding his saddlebag and bedroll over his right shoulder and picking up his carbine, Hardy marched into the kitchen.

Emma greeted him with a tin of coffee.

He downed the hot liquid quickly, gave her the cup, then started for the door. "I'll saddle my horse."

"Wait!" She scurried to the door and grabbed a lantern and tin of matches from the adjacent corner where a shotgun was propped against the wall. "Here take these so you can see."

He accepted the lantern and the matches tin, then she moved closer to him, standing on her tiptoes and reaching for his head. He thought she was going to kiss him, but her hands took his hat by the brim and lifted it off his head.

She smiled bashfully. "I will keep this here. I do not want you riding off without breakfast." Emma opened the door and let him outside.

The day was at its darkest and was brisk with the spring cool. Hardy moved quickly to the barn, lit the lantern and saw his gray stamping in the stall. The gelding was tossing his head with the anticipation of a run.

Quickly, Hardy bridled and saddled the animal, then cinched down his saddlebags and bedroll. He hooked his carbine scabbard in place, the stock sticking up over the rump of his horse. He didn't linger, wanting to spend as much time with Emma as he could before dawn. Taking the reins, he led the gelding to the barn door, then blew out the lantern and marched back to the house. He tied the reins to the porch and stepped back into the kitchen. It was as warm as Emma's smile.

At his place at the table sat a tin plate piled high with flapjacks and fried bacon. She picked up the coffeepot with a pot holder and poured him a fresh cup, which she set beside his plate. As he eased into his chair, she shoved a jug of cane syrup and a bowl of butter at him. While he slathered his pancakes with butter and syrup, she eased around the table and took the chair opposite him.

"Aren't you eating?" Hardy pointed with his fork at the empty place before her.

Emma smiled. "I'll have all day to eat, but only a few more moments to watch you."

Hardy felt his face flush. He was as embarrassed by her sentiment as he was desirous of her charms. He attacked the pancakes.

"You are a fine man, Doyle Hardy."

His face flushed hotter. "Surprised you think so after what the LeHew brothers said about me."

"You mean the brothel?"

He nodded. "I'm a married man."

"I know," she said, "and I also know the lies bad men tell. They lie most about lawmen and women, especially the bad kind."

"I just wanted you to know that I didn't attack any girl at any brothel."

"You are the man that saved my sons. Such a man would be no less decent with young ladies or his wife."

Hardy averted his eyes, focusing on his diminishing stack of pancakes. He did not know what to say so he said nothing, filling his mouth with another bite of flapjacks and bacon. His silence said more than words could manage.

"Does she love you?"

Hardy shook his head. "She once did."

"She is a fool if she no longer does," Emma told him.

"We share a son," Hardy managed, "but I am not so certain any more that is enough, not with what Bud has done."

He said nothing more and Emma pressed him no further, merely watching him eat and filling his coffee cup each time he emptied it.

Hardy wanted to stay longer, but through the window he could see the sky beginning to pale outside. He must leave before dawn. He scraped a final bite of bacon and syrup, then washed it down with the last of his coffee. Emma moved for the pot but he held up his hand. She answered with lips that tottered between a smile and a grimace.

"Be careful, Doyle Hardy."

"And you be careful as well. Do you have a weapon?"

She nodded. "The shotgun by the door and a revolver at my bed."

He pushed himself away from the table. She stood quickly and went to the door, taking his hat from the hook where she had hung it.

"Thank you, Emma. You saved my life."

She shook her head. "You would have survived. It is I who owe you the thanks. You saved my sons."

He stepped toward her and she stood on her toes, placing his hat like a crown upon his head as he bowed his neck to her.

"Take care of the little ones."

"Take care of yourself."

There was an awkward moment between them when neither seemed to know what to do. Hardy reached for her hand and shook it, then opened the door. He did not look back, but as he tried to shut the door he felt resistance and knew she held it open.

He marched outside, mounted quickly and turned the gray from the house without glancing at the door. He nudged the gray's flank with his boot and started for the front of the house. Out of the corner of his eyes he saw Emma Sims, silhouetted in the door. He kicked his gelding into a trot and rounded the house, aiming for the Boggy Depot Road while it was still dark.

With the LeHew brothers still searching for him, Hardy decided to follow the road as long as the cover of darkness lasted. Then he would swing wide of the road to reduce the odds of a chance encounter with the LeHews. As he turned toward Boggy Depot, he slapped the reins against the neck of his horse, then leaned into the saddle and pulled his hat down as the powerful gelding stretched his strides into a gallop.

The morning was quiet with only the pounding of the gray's hooves to disturb the tranquility. Behind him to the east, the pink stain of morning began to creep over the trees and push away the darkness. The morning air, fragrant with the scent of pine, was cool against his face as the gelding dashed along the trail. Freed of the Sims's barn, the gray seemed to relish the run, its head moving rhythmically with its stride.

As the darkness gradually gave way to dawn's soft light, murky through the trees, Hardy loosened his hold on the reins. The more Hardy let off on the reins, the greater speed the gelding pulled from its reserve until its muscled flesh rippled with power. By good light the gelding was running at top speed along the trail and approaching Willow Creek. The gelding resisted Hardy's slight drag on the reins, throwing his head against the halter as if he could shake himself free. Hardy tugged harder and the horse gave in reluctantly, gradually easing off but not before splashing through the gravelly bottom of Willow Creek.

Hardy cried out with surprise at the shock of the cold water splattering his face and clothes. With a strong tug on the reins, Hardy convinced the gelding to ease off and gradually the gray slipped into a trot, then a walk, tossing and shaking his head. To the south of the road two miles ahead stood Signal Hill. Between the creek and Signal Hill was the location of the still Newt and Tate Sims had wanted Hardy to check out. Hardy eased off the road into the trees and began to make a wide circle south of the trail. He wouldn't tarry long looking for the bootleggers because he was not likely to find them at the still. He would, though, make a search and destroy the still if he could find it, but he doubted that would be enough to scare off the moonshiners for good.

After moving south of the trail for fifteen minutes, Hardy turned the gelding west and moved parallel to the Boggy Depot Road. He looked for trails that the moonshiners might take to reach their still or for the brush arbors they would use to hide it. He found nothing at first, but when he saw the ears of the gray flick forward, he pulled back on the reins and sat silently among the trees. The gelding had heard something.

Hardy listened until the horse's ears relaxed, then he nudged the horse ahead. The horse had carried him a quarter of a mile farther west when Hardy picked up the noise. It was a soft thumping noise that seemed to be diffused by the trees, coming from nowhere yet from everywhere at the same time. At first Hardy could not identify it and he let the gelding advance slowly.

The thumping sound gradually grew more distinct and Hardy knew he was drawing nearer the noise. The thump became a loud whack that almost echoed through the trees. It was the sound of someone chopping wood. Maybe it was someone cutting trees for fence posts, maybe it was someone chopping firewood or maybe it was someone hewing wood to fuel a still.

This early in the day, Hardy figured it had to be moonshiners at work brewing up another batch of poison for sale in Choctaw Nation. Hardy twisted around in the saddle and pulled his carbine from its leather sheath. He rested the barrel of his Winchester in the crook of his elbow, then guided the gelding toward the sound. The woods were thick, offering cover to his advantage but screening the woodchopper to Hardy's disadvantage.

The whacking noise continued at a steady rhythm. Hardy caught a flash of movement in the woods just thirty feet away and swung his carbine around, but the threat was only a bluejay startled from its perch. Hardy relaxed for an instant, then froze at the sound of a dry branch snapping beneath the hooves of his gray. The chopping continued undisturbed, seeming to be ever closer. Deciding he had ridden close enough, Hardy pulled back on the reins, the gray stopping in its tracks. The saddle creaked as Hardy dismounted.

For a moment, the chopping stopped and Hardy heard voices. Hardy froze until the woodcutting resumed, then tied the reins around the trunk of a pine tree. He crouched and moved toward the noise, advancing quietly on the bed of pine needles.

He had advanced no more than a dozen yards from his horse when the gray whinnied.

The woodcutting stopped.

"Who's there?" came a voice, followed by a gun-shot that whizzed through the trees.

Hardy waited a moment, then inched forward. Through a break in the trees up ahead, he finally saw a muscular black man, his shirtless chest glistening with sweat. Holding his ax like he was ready to defend himself, he revolved slowly around on his heels, trying to identify what had caused the noise.

Hardy peeked around a tree, trying to spot the black man's partner who had evidently fired the shot. Beyond the black man, he saw the back of a wagon and beyond it a brush arbor, which Hardy knew screened a still. Hardy advanced tree by tree, gradually getting a broader view of the moonshiner camp and finally spotting the second moonshiner, standing on the wagon seat, rifle in hand.

Though the Sims brothers had mentioned only two moonshiners, there could be others. Hardy weighed whether to throw down on the two men now and risk not seeing another partner or whether to wait a moment longer and risk losing sight of both of them. He decided to act. If they resisted, he would kill them, but he preferred to take them prisoner and then release them with a message for other moon-shiners: anybody operating a still or selling liquor within ten miles of Emma Sims's house did so at risk of his life.

Hardy knelt behind a tree and aimed his carbine at the man in the wagon. "Drop your weapons and reach for the treetops."

The two men flinched with surprise, then stiff-ened as they considered resistance.

"This is a Deputy U.S. Marshal ordering you to drop your weapons."

Both moonshiners looked around, their gaze missing

Hardy initially. "Says who?" called the white man with the rifle.

"Says Doyle Hardy, Deputy Marshal, Western District of Arkansas."

"Don't want no trouble with Doyle Hardy," said the black man, pitching his ax to the ground and raising his hand. "He's the son of a bitch that's out to kill his own son."

The white man in the wagon tossed his rifle to the ground. "If he'd do that, he'd kill us as easy as spit."

11

Hardy slipped from behind the tree, his Winchester level at his waist and aimed at the two moonshiners. They were both big men, their eyes darting from side to side as they watched Hardy approach. Hardy motioned with the carbine for the white man to climb down from the wagon.

"Keep your hands where I can see them," Hardy commanded.

Cautiously, the man eased over the side of the wagon and edged toward his black companion, who stood over a tree they had downed and dragged to the still with the wagon team.

Emerging from the trees into a natural clearing, Hardy took in the surroundings and the still through an opening in the brush arbor. The two horses staked to the ground lifted their heads from the new grass, then resumed their grazing beside a narrow stream that skirted the still.

Something bothered Hardy about his exchange with the moonshiners. He couldn't figure it out until he realized the men knew things they shouldn't know. "Who said I was out to kill my son?"

The two men looked at one another, then shook their heads.

"Why should we tell you?" the black man spat out.

"Cause rumor suggests I might kill the two of you if you don't."

Both men gulped.

"It'd be murder," the white man shot back.

Hardy gave them a narrow grin. "Who would know?" Hardy observed the black moonshiner eyeing the ax on the ground. Swinging the carbine toward the ax, Hardy squeezed off a round. The bullet thudded off the steel head of the ax and whizzed through the trees, groaning as it went. Both men flinched, then gritted their teeth.

"Of course, if you tell me I just might let the two of you go."

The white man started to speak but his partner grabbed his arm.

"You can't trust a man that would kill his own boy."

"You don't have a choice," Hardy told him. "And, shut your mouth unless I ask a question." Hardy waved the gun at the black man's nose. "What's your name?"

The black man licked his lips. "Homer Tally."

"And yours?" Hardy swung the gun around to the white man.

"Calvin Baker's my name."

Hardy raked them over with his steel gray eyes. "One more chance, Calvin. Now tell me who said I was out to kill my son?"

"Will you let us go?"

"I sure won't if you don't."

Baker looked to Tally for a moment, then coughed nervously. "It was your boy himself."

"How do you know it was him?"

"He said so. I didn't have no reason to doubt him."

"Describe him," Hardy instructed.

The black man stamped his feet and grumbled. "We don't need to be telling nothing to the law."

Baker twisted his head to Tally. "It's our only chance of staying out of Judge Parker's jail."

Hardy stepped to Tally and poked the carbine barrel in his flat stomach. "Shut up." Hardy cut his gaze to Baker, "Now describe him."

"Long brown hair, over the ears. Fancy dresser, wearing a derby hat and twin Colt revolvers, long-barreled with ivory handles."

Baker was telling the truth. Bud Hardy was as vain as any man who ever rode Indian Territory. "Where'd you see Bud?"

Before Baker could answer, Tally spoke up, evidently deciding to cooperate as well before his partner spilled all the information. "Just past Eastman's Mill. Sold him two jugs of liquor."

"If he thinks I'm out to kill him, why's he talking so much, rather than getting out of the territory?"

Baker shrugged. "Way I figure it, he thinks you have enough enemies in Choctaw Nation that one will get you if he just let them know you were coming to begin with."

Knowing how Bud thought, Hardy admitted that was a plausible explanation. "Was Bud riding alone?"

"We heard he had been seen with the LeHew brothers, but we didn't see them," Tally offered.

"He did buy two jugs, though," interjected Baker. "That's a lot of liquor for one man."

Hardy nodded. Bud didn't drink all the time, but when he did, he could sure polish away the joy juice before getting rip-snorting drunk. With Eastman's Mill just four easy riding hours away, Hardy thought he might be able to catch up with Bud and arrest him tonight. "Why's Bud lingering at Eastman's Mill?"

Baker shrugged. "He bragged he had been seeing a young lady, and needed a little more time with her."

Tally explained further. "Last word he had was you'd been shot, though they didn't find your body. He was hanging around for the girl and news of your death. He said it didn't matter how big a lead he got on you because you were a shrewd one who could pick up a trail as easy as a hound picks up fleas. No sense in running too hard from that type of lawman, he said."

His son was right. Hardy would ultimately catch up with Bud, no matter where he went. Then Hardy remembered another of U.S. Marshal Jacob Yoes's damned rules. *No transfer of warrants between deputies will be permitted without the knowledge and consent of the marshal.* Damn if Bud wasn't a shrewd one. If Hardy were bushwhacked, it would take time for another deputy to get the warrant and take up the trail, plenty of time for Bud to leave the territory. No wonder Bud was telling everybody his father planned to kill him and putting a five hundred dollar reward on Hardy's head.

"Did Bud make you any offers to kill me?"

The two men nodded. "Five hundred dollars," said Baker.

"How was he to know you or anyone else killed me?"

Tally replied, "Whoever killed you was to take all your papers and your badge to him. Whoever killed you could keep all your money and things as long as he got the papers and badge."

Hardy let out a long slow breath and bit his lip.

Damn, if Bud wasn't a dangerous and vicious man. It was enough to turn his stomach. Hardy saw the two moonshiners quiver before his suddenly hardened gaze.

"You ain't gonna kill us, are you?" Tally asked, nervously shifting from foot to foot.

Hardy pulled the gun barrel from the black man's belly and backed up. "I told you I'd let you go."

Tally smiled narrowly.

Baker nodded. "We'll just gather our stuff and go on."

Hardy shook his head. "Not quite, boys. I'll let you go after you destroy your still and your wagon."

"What?" they shouted in unison.

"Our still, okay," cried Baker, "but not the wagon."

Again, Hardy shook his head and pointed the barrel of the carbine at the ax. "If I leave the still you boys will come back in a few days. If I let you take the wagon, you'll likely set up somewhere nearby." Hardy intended to keep his promise to the Sims boys and run the moonshiners away for good. "I don't want you setting up your still or selling whiskey within ten miles of this spot. Otherwise, I'll kill you. Understood?"

Both men nodded reluctantly.

"I thought you'd see the wisdom in my offer."

Hardy waved his carbine at the ax. "Tally, get the ax and take to chopping up your still."

The black man lowered his hands and moved slowly for the ax.

"You do anything I think is a threat, I'll shoot you."

He nodded as he picked up the ax, then trod to the brush arbor that screened the still. It was a simple still with a capped iron boiler sitting atop a platform rock firebox. From the top of the boiler a metal tube stretched toward a nearby wooden barrel. The tubing sloped into the barrel and twisted into a coil that was submerged in the water-filled barrel. A drain tube at the bottom of the barrel ended in a funnel that emptied into a brown jug. It took a lot of work to build a still and keep it hidden. Hardy knew why Tally hesitated to demolish it.

"Start tearing it up," Hardy ordered.

The moonshiner hefted the ax above his head and swung it for the barrel, gashing a hole between staves. Water began to gush out.

"Go on and demolish it."

Tally began to swing the ax rhythmically, chopping at the barrel until it was nothing but kindling and the tubing was exposed like a metal skeleton.

"Chop the worm in pieces," Hardy commanded and Tally began to swing at the metal coil.

His ax bounced off the tubing, bending but not cutting the metal, until he hit the condensation pipe near the top of the furnace, severing it from the still itself. Then Tally kicked the coiled tubing toward the rock platform for a solid cutting surface as he swung the ax at the metal worm, snapping it in pieces as the ax blade cut through the tubing and dulled itself on the rock. Next Tally attacked the furnace, hammering at it with the blunted end of the ax blade. The bang of metal against metal reverberated through the woods. Tally threw all his anger as well as his weight and energy into each ax swing until his torso glistened with sweat.

When he was done, the metal still was so beaten and battered that it could not be repaired. Tally took a deep breath, panted for a moment, then turned to Hardy. "That good enough for you?"

"It'll do," Hardy answered. "Now real easy, toss your ax over to Baker. Let's see how he handles a blade."

The winded moonshiner pitched the ax at his partner. Baker squatted to retrieve the tool. He arose slowly, a disbelieving look upon his face. "I'm not gonna chop apart the whole wagon?"

Hardy shook his head. "Just knock the spokes out of each wheel until the wagon is sitting on its hubs."

Baker grimaced.

"It's that or a ride to Fort Smith."

Drawing back the ax, Baker aimed for the bottom spoke of the rear wheel. As he swung for the wagon wheel, he cursed. The dull blade landed with a thud and a crack. He alternated between the bottom spokes, then the top spokes, gradually knocking away neighboring spokes until only the side spokes supported the hub. Then as he began to chop at them, the remaining pair of spokes began to sag and quiver under the weight of the wagon. Then with a loud snap, the final spokes gave and the corner of the wagon drooped to the ground.

Hardy followed Baker from wheel to wheel, watching him and Tally all the while. The second and the third wheels were soon destroyed and only a front corner kept the wagon off all four hubs. As Hardy trailed Baker, he stopped and picked up the moonshiner's discarded rifle and tossed it into the woods out of reach.

Baker took a deep breath, sweat beading on his forehead as he began his reluctant attack on the final wheel. His face was red with exertion and rage as the final spokes snapped and the wagon thudded to the ground, the hubs digging into the soft soil. The wagon wheels were nothing but wire-rimmed hoops, useless forever.

Nodding that the work had been accomplished, Hardy motioned with his index finger for the two men to move to each other's side. "Now, let's march back into the woods."

The two men looked at each other, a touch of panic in their knowing gazes.

"You're gonna kill us now, aren't you?" Tally said, then turned to Baker. "I told you we couldn't trust him."

"Shut up," Hardy demanded. "You'll go with me back to my horse and lead me back toward the road before I let you go."

With his elbow Baker nudged Tally in the ribs. "Let it lie before you get us killed."

Tally's shoulders slumped. The black man followed Baker into the woods, Hardy trailing them, telling them which way to turn to get back to his gelding.

As they approached the horse, Hardy ordered them to give him room to mount. They did as he said and he untied his horse and quickly pulled himself into the saddle. He escorted them again to the camp and had them wait while he let his gelding take a drink from the narrow stream.

"Boys, I guess you better lead me a half mile or so toward the road, just so I'll know you won't be shooting at my back."

They grumbled.

"What was that?" Hardy challenged.

They both shrugged and started for the road.

Hardy let the gray gelding fall in behind them, reining him back occasionally to keep him from overtaking the two reluctant hikers.

"Would you really kill your own boy?" Tally asked.

Hardy spat on the trail. "My job is to bring back a man accused of murdering his wife and boy."

"But would you kill him?"

"I'll do whatever it takes to get him to a trial. The courts'll decide if he dies, not me. But if he decides to resist, he's committing suicide."

"Damn, you're a mean one," Baker said.

Hardy nodded. "You boys better remember that because if I ever catch you around here with a still or a bottle of liquor, I'll kill you."

"We ain't forgot," Tally answered.

"Good thing, boys," Hardy said. "Now let me pass."

The two moonshiners moved out of his way and Hardy sent the gray into a canter past them. He could hear their curses sending him on his way.

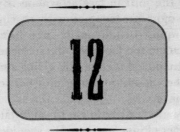

12

Doyle Hardy skirted the edge of the Boggy Depot Road, riding twenty to thirty yards off the trail to avoid the passing riders and occasional wagons. He was particularly alert any time he saw three riders for they could be the LeHew brothers. Once the two moonshiners reached the road, they would spread word of his location. If the LeHew brothers weren't in the vicinity, they soon would be. Hardy wondered what type of lies the moonshiners would spread about him. Manufacturing lies about a deputy's integrity was one way the lawless element got back at the law officers. Hardy figured he would be accused of drinking their liquor and stealing their money. Of course, that might sound more logical than him forcing them to destroy their wagon.

It was past midmorning when Hardy turned deeper into the woods and rode the gray atop Signal Hill. The hill was the highest vantage point for miles and would give him a chance to survey the territory before moving to Eastman's Mill. With Bud seen just yesterday at Eastman's Mill, Hardy planned to approach the mill in late afternoon. By then Bud might be more preoccupied with chasing a skirt or finding liquor. Liquor made men like Bud more adventuresome and foolhardy, but it also reduced their reflexes and dulled their minds, giving a sober man an edge in the cat-and-mouse games between lawmen and outlaws.

Hardy guided the horse through tall pines and over a carpet of pine needles. His shoulder still ached from the shotgun blast it had absorbed, but the stiffness in his muscles bothered him more. After four days and nights, spent mostly in Emma Sims's bed, his muscles had rusted and turned stubborn on him, not responding as quickly as he would like. That could be dangerous in this line of work, but damn if he didn't enjoy it more than grubbing potatoes or chopping weeds on his farm. Hardy wondered how much the thought of Tinnie accounted for his dour outlook on farming.

Even so, law enforcement was a young man's game, at least physically. Hardy wasn't so sure mentally. Physical skills, for the most part, came naturally. Mental acuity, though, was acquired. Looking back over his career, Hardy figured the wisdom acquired by experience was what had kept him alive, not the physical strength and bravado that he would have credited twenty or more years ago. Wisdom, though, wasn't salve to his aching muscles as the gray topped Signal Hill.

Atop the hill, Hardy dismounted. He hobbled the gray and let it blow, then graze as he studied the road below, noting a few riders, but none in a group of three, as well as a handful of farm wagons inching along the hard-packed trail. In the distance, he spotted Eastman's Mill beside the rambling river which powered the mill.

Hardy turned from his observation post and ambled toward a tall pine tree that offered a bit of shade. He sat down and leaned back against the base of the tree to take a nap. Pulling his hat down over his eyes, he dozed for half an hour. When he arose, he stretched his arms and shook his legs to rid them of their stiffness. He moved over to the gray, unhobbled the gelding, then mounted and started down the hill.

By midafternoon, Hardy was hidden in the perimeter trees around Eastman's Mill, studying the six buildings that made up the community. In addition to the mill itself, the burg had a couple of wooden cabins, a small store, a cramped building that offered overnight accommodations for men willing to share a bed and a final building where Hardy suspected men could buy a woman companion or a drink on the sly. Hardy figured this unmarked building with two horses outside switching at flies was where Homer Tally and Calvin Baker had been selling their contraband whiskey. Neither of the horses was Bud's nor were they the mounts of the LeHew brothers. Beyond the town, the Boggy Depot Road crossed a plank bridge wide enough for a single wagon to pass.

Hardy heard the whine of a whirling blade from the sawmill, then the groan as the metal teeth bit into the wood. Hardy reached for the marshal's badge on his chest and unpinned it, sliding it in his trouser's pocket as he slowly straightened in his saddle. Then Hardy nudged his horse forward, emerging from the trees and angling across the clearing past a house where a woman was removing clothes from a clothesline strung between the corner of her house and a single pine tree in back. She stopped for a moment and stared at him as he rode to the mill. Dismounting, then tying the gray's reins to a hitching ring, Hardy stared at her until she started minding her own business again. Then he entered the mill door, which merely opened up on a small vestibule with a stairway leading up to a second level. Hardy climbed the stairs, emerging on a planked deck covered with sawdust.

Foggy with sawdust spewing from a spinning, three-foot blade as it bit into a thick pine log, the room opened to a loading ramp where a sturdy farm wagon was being loaded with lumber. Opposite Hardy, large shutters opened out onto the river and Hardy could see the turning of the waterwheel as it slapped against the water. The gears and pulleys on the waterwheel's axle drove wide leather belts that powered the huge blade.

Hardy stood for a couple of minutes before either of the two men working the saw or the other two loading the wagon noticed. When the mill operator finally looked up from his blade, he nodded his acknowledgment, then finished sawing the log into planks, which his handlers loaded into the wagon. When he was done, the mill operator pulled a lever, the leather belt sliding off the drum that turned the blade. The whirring growl of the blade died slowly, being replaced by the slap of the wide leather drive belt as it whipped against the pulleys. When the mill operator jerked another lever and set the brake, the leather belt sagged and died after expending the last of its momentum.

"Howdy," yelled the mill operator as if he were still trying to shout over the dying machinery. The operator shook sawdust from his hair as he stepped around the saw blade and the log bed. He was a slight man with red watery eyes and a runny nose. He pulled a kerchief from his bib overalls and wiped at his eyes and nose. As he held the kerchief, Hardy noticed that the tips of the three longest fingers on his left hand reached only to the tip of his little finger, likely the result of a sawmill accident.

As the man stuffed his kerchief back in his pocket, he cocked his head and pointed the shortened index finger of his left hand at Hardy.

"You ain't wearing a badge," he said as he came within reach and offered Hardy his right hand, "but you're that marshal, Doyle Hardy."

Hardy nodded, shaking his hand.

"There's a lean look about you deputies, that and something in your eyes, a meanness. I guess you're as easy to spot as a man that's done any work for long with lumber." The man held up his left hand and wiggled his shortened fingers. "That gives me away every time."

"I didn't catch your name."

"Pernell Eastman," the mill operator replied.

"How'd you know I was Doyle Hardy?"

"A younger fellow's been coming here to the store, taking nights at the place across the road. He's long brown hair, a bit cocky, and wearing two Colts with ivory grips on them. Says you would be coming after him."

"Did he tell you why I was coming after him?"

Eastman scratched his chin, prickly with whiskers. "Said he was blamed for murdering his wife and boy."

Hardy nodded. "He was blamed because he did it."

"He ain't my type and he damn sure ain't Jim Boykin's type."

"Boykin, who's he?"

"A farmer a couple miles across the river. The young fellow's taken a fancy to Boykin's daughter, Connie. The old man don't like him none."

"The old man's right," Hardy replied. "You don't know where the young fellow is, do you?"

"I ain't seen him in a while, but he's got folks looking for you, promising five hundred dollars for your hide. Three fellows, in particular, have been looking for you around here the past couple days. Word has it they're brothers."

"You wouldn't tell them I was around, now would you?"

Vigorously, Eastman shook his head. "I won't. I do know this, Jim Boykin would be mighty glad to see the young fellow leave. He's fearful for his daughter."

With good reason, Hardy thought, considering what Bud did to his wife and son. "Where's the Boykin place?"

"Two miles past the river bridge, his place is about a half mile south of the road. There's a trail leading to his house. It's marked with a pine tree with a letter *B* in the bark."

Hardy nodded. "Obliged."

Eastman gave Hardy a puzzled look. "Is it true he's your boy?"

Taking a deep breath, Hardy stroked his chin. He nodded slightly. "He is, I'm ashamed to admit."

Eastman shook his head. "I hope things work out for you."

Hardy sighed. "As long as no innocent parties get hurt again, it will."

Turning around, Hardy marched back down the stairs and outside to his gelding. He swatted at his coat to brush away the sawdust which had settled on it. Untying the reins from the hitching ring, he led the horse across the road to the store. It was a small log building with a solid wooden door and not a single window, likely to prevent theft. The store was identified only by a plank that was nailed to the wall. Someone had painted *Mercantile* across the plank.

Hardy tied his horse to a vacant hitching post and looked both ways down the road. He saw nothing coming and no one watching except the curious woman finishing laundry behind her house. Hardy stopped, crossed his arms over his shoulder and stared back. She turned quickly back to her own business. Then Hardy pushed open the thick door.

In the murky light of a single, low-burning lamp, Hardy could just make out an old man slowly pushing himself from a stool in the corner. The old man looked as old as his goods stacked on makeshift shelves made from scrap lumber from the mill. Along a side wall, the storekeeper had a bed and a heating stove that he evidently used for cooking his meals from the looks of the pan and skillet atop it.

When he finally managed to get to his feet, the old man swayed in the corner like a tall tree in a light breeze. "Need something?"

As his eyes adjusted to the dimness, Hardy studied the canned goods against the side wall. Tables of cloth goods, tinware, cast-iron cookery and leather goods stood in the middle of the floor and behind them at the back of the room was a small glass display counter with a pair of knives, some sewing goods and some cheap trinkets that passed for jewelry.

Hardy marched over to the canned goods. "You got any canned tomatoes and peaches?" Hardy figured those would do for supper.

"Used to have some," the storekeeper said, his voice as wobbly as his step as he started across the room.

Scanning the shelves, Hardy found a half dozen tins marked TOMATOES but by the bloated cans he knew they were spoiled. He found a single can of peaches and took it from the shelf.

"You found them?" the old man wheezed.

"Found the peaches."

"Used to be some tomatoes up there."

"This'll do," Hardy replied, reaching in his pocket for a coin.

He strode to the old man, placing two bits in his hand.

"Peaches is it? That'll be a dime." The old man held the quarter between his thumb and forefinger and studied it in what little light the single lamp threw off. "I ain't got change for two bits. You wanna buy something else?"

Hardy didn't see anything worth buying. "Nope."

"I ain't got change for two bits," the old man repeated. "You wanna buy something else?"

"No, sir," he said loudly. "Just give me a receipt for the two bits."

The old man looked from the coin to Hardy. "A receipt? You must be law. No strangers but law ask for receipts." The old man retreated for the counter and Hardy thought it would take forever.

When the proprietor finally reached the counter and shuffled around behind it, he couldn't find his pencil and paper. He looked all around until Hardy pointed it out to him on the counter beside his hands.

"Oops," the old man apologized, "my eyesight's not what it once was." He began to scrawl out a receipt, his feeble hand trembling from the exertion.

Hardy began to wonder if the man would finish the receipt by the end of the month. Finally, the proprietor put down his pencil, held up his sheet of paper and read it to himself, then he offered it to Hardy, who quickly scanned it. The old man wrote down a can for ten cents rather than a quarter. Hardy didn't know if he would outlive another attempt by the man to write a receipt. He nodded. "Thanks."

"Any time," answered the proprietor, "but I think I've still got some tomatoes up there if you want to look."

"Not this trip, old-timer," Hardy answered, going out the door. He looked both ways down the road and saw the woman at the adjacent cabin taking in some of her clothes. She stared for a moment, then quickly averted her gaze when she saw Hardy looking at her.

Untying his horse, Hardy mounted and headed for the narrow plank bridge across the river. The sawmill was still whining as his horse clippity-clopped across the bridge. He stayed on the road until he came to a trail that pointed to a farm house. The trail was marked by a pine with a *B* blazed in its bark.

Hardy eased off the road, pleased he had encountered no one since leaving Eastman's Mill. Rather than follow the trail, Hardy eased into the trees and skirted the trail. He preferred to study the place before approaching it. With luck, he might catch Bud coming to call on Connie Boykin. Hardy guided the horse through the trees until he could see the Boykin's house, barn and field. By looking at them, Hardy could tell Boykin was an industrious man. Knee-high corn, taller than any Hardy had seen on the trail, stood in precise rows in his fields. His garden was full of vegetables and he even had an orchard of a half dozen apple and peach trees. In a corral by the barn were several cows and horses. Hardy studied the horses to see if he saw Bud's pinto. He didn't.

Except for the smoke coming from the stovepipe, Hardy saw little sign of activity. He touched his boot heel to the gray and moved a little deeper into the woods where he dismounted, tied his horse and fished his pocketknife from his britches. It was a knife fit for skinning a deer or slicing a man. He pulled open its sharply honed, six-inch blade and stabbed it into the top of the canned peaches and began to slice through the metal. He gradually peeled back the lid, lifted the tin to his lips and drank the sweet syrup. Then he forked the peach slices with his knife and ate them slowly.

When he was done, he tossed the tin can away, folded his knife and slipped it into his pocket, then seated himself by a tree to watch the Boykin place. It didn't make much sense, as clean a place as the man kept that someone was not out doing some kind of work today. Of course, Hardy had lost track of days since he was shot and wasn't certain what day of the week it was.

Maybe his plan had been a bad one, waiting until late in the afternoon to approach the place. But if Bud was drinking—and where else but liquor could a man who had murdered his wife and son turn?—he might be easier to take if he were inebriated. Hardy scoffed. Bud didn't have the grit to be a tough man, though he tried to act the part.

Doyle Hardy dug into his pants pocket and pulled out the badge he had removed before Eastman's Mill. He pinned it to his broadcloth coat, then slowly pushed himself to his feet. He brushed the pine needles off his pants and glanced at the gray nuzzling at the grass. He considered riding the horse up to the place, but decided to leave it hidden in the trees. If Bud were to approach while the horse was outside, he would recognize it and escape.

As he emerged from the trees, Hardy uncovered his revolver and hooked his broadcloth coat behind his pistol butt. He wriggled the fingers of his gun hand, then massaged them with his left hand. The sun was just dropping behind the trees, so the long shadows helped cover Hardy's approach. Reaching the front porch without drawing any attention from the house, he stood in silence. He could hear voices from inside. His muscles tensed at the sound of one voice. It sounded like Bud.

Now he had a problem, should he barge in and risk hurting innocent people or let Bud dictate the encounter. Hardy didn't care for that option, but he felt it was safer for the innocent. He would play dumb. He stepped on the porch, the wood creaking under his weight. The conversation from inside the house went silent.

Hardy knocked on the door, then stood to the side hugging the wall so he could not be seen through the window.

Receiving no answer though people were certainly inside, Hardy knocked again.

A voice from inside answered. "Who is it?"

"Deputy Marshal Doyle Hardy. I need to speak to the owner." Hardy could just barely make out hushed whispers from inside.

"We ain't done nothing," came the same male voice.

"Nobody says you have. My horse stepped in a rabbit hole, broke his leg down the road. I had to shoot him and need a horse. I'd buy or borrow him from you."

The door quivered and the handle slowly turned before the door parted enough for a man to stick his head outside.

He was a sandy-headed man, middle-aged and nervous. He twisted his head until he saw Hardy.

"I wondered how you slipped up here without us hearing."

"Don't mean to be a bother," Hardy apologized, stepping in front of the door and trying to see past the man he took to be Boykin. "I'm Doyle Hardy."

"Boykin's my name. You're on my place." Boykin opened the door enough to slip outside, then quickly shut it behind him. Boykin was a tall man, made lean by years of hard work. He had eyes that were dulled with fear. "Sorry about your horse."

Hardy nodded. "It's a shame. I was on the tail of a murderer named Bud Hardy." Hardy decided to fire both barrels of the accusations. "Damn shame he's gonna get away from me. He's a dangerous man, killed his young wife and baby boy, his own son, mind you."

Boykin grimaced, glancing furtively over his shoulder, then biting his lip.

The farmer was a poor poker player, Hardy thought, letting his hand move casually closer to the butt of his Colt .45. The man was too nervous not to be sheltering Bud.

"Ain't seen him," Boykin lied, then stared at Hardy, his eyes showing the fear.

At that moment came a scream from inside.

Boykin went pale, but Hardy jumped past him, drawing his handgun and barging through the door. He saw a Choctaw woman sprawled on the floor and nothing else!

Bud had escaped out the back!

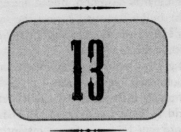

13

Doyle Hardy ran through the kitchen and burst out the back door, drawing his Colt as he bounced off the porch and ran to the waist-high cistern wall for cover. Glancing around, he caught a movement as the barn door closed. He aimed his pistol at the barn.

Hearing a commotion behind him, Hardy checked over his shoulder as Boykin flew out the door.

"He's got Connie! He'll hurt her," Boykin screamed, charging headlong for the barn.

Hardy lunged and tackled the panicked father, then dragged him to the base of the cistern.

"He's a mean one," Boykin blabbered. "He threatened us if we didn't let him see Connie."

"Shut up," Hardy barked, just as he heard a bang at the barn door. He peeked around the side of the cistern and saw Bud bolting out of the barn on his pinto.

Hardy took aim with his pistol, his finger tightening against the trigger. He grimaced then diverted his aim. Connie Boykin was riding behind Bud. Hardy couldn't risk injuring her.

Though Hardy hesitated, Bud squeezed off a shot at him. The bullet slammed against the stone cistern, splattering Hardy and Boykin with bits of rock, which peppered their faces.

"He's got my girl," Boykin yelled, then jumped up, making himself a better target.

Hardy grabbed Boykin by the belt, jerking him to the ground as Bud fired again. In that moment, Hardy's gaze met his son's for an instant. Bud's eyes burned with the arrogant pride Hardy had first seen when he had surprised the boy with his first horse. Hardy had seen the same haughty pride when Bud recounted killing Rube Bell. But now there was in Bud's eyes a meanness that Hardy had never seen or, at least, never recognized before.

The bullet from Bud's gun whizzed harmlessly over Boykin and Hardy as they fell to the ground. Then Bud shot past the house, the horse galloping as fast as it could under the weight of two riders.

Hardy ran to the corner of the house and watched the horse charge down the trail, then turn down the road toward Boggy Depot.

Boykin was up, screaming in panic. "He's stolen my girl, he's stolen my girl."

Hardy shoved his pistol back in his holster. "He'll leave her after a couple miles."

"He's stolen my girl." Boykin cried out hysterically.

Grabbing Boykin by the shirt, Hardy shoved him up against the house. "Listen to me," he growled. "He won't take her far. He let her ride with him to cover his back so I wouldn't shoot at him."

"The bastard."

"Now listen to me, I'll get my horse and catch him."

Boykin looked perplexed. "I thought your horse was dead."

"It was a ruse to get to the house unseen. You saddle a horse and follow. We'll find your girl down the road a ways."

Just as Hardy turned away from Boykin he saw in the kitchen door the woman who he had seen on the parlor floor. She was rubbing her head. She was a Choctaw like Emma Sims, but nowhere as pretty.

"Your girl'll be okay," Hardy assured her as he bolted toward the woods and his gray gelding.

Reaching his horse, Hardy untied him and clambered into the saddle. The horse danced and stamped nervously until Hardy nudged him. He started forward at an easy trot, weaving through the trees to the Boykin trail, then galloping toward the road. Instinctively, the horse turned down the road toward Boggy Depot. In spite of Bud's lead, Hardy knew his gray could catch Bud's mount. Bud had bought the pinto because it was a showy horse that caught men's eyes, not because it had good speed or endurance.

Hardy gave his gray free rein for two miles, but he drew up on the leather when he rounded a curve in the road and saw a dress-clad body ahead. For a moment, he feared the worst, then he saw some movement and heard sobs as he approached. He halted the horse beside her and jumped from the saddle, hanging onto the reins as he squatted over her.

Connie Boykin was twitching and crying with grief. She stared at Hardy with the dark eyes of her mother and ran her fingers through her long black hair.

"He threw me off," she explained through the tears and sobs. "Said he loved me, then shoved me to the ground without slowing."

"Anything broken?"

Connie seemed to focus on him for the first time.

"Let me help you up." He grabbed her high on the arm and assisted her to a sitting position, then to her feet.

She stared at him a moment. Instead of thanking him, though, she asked a question. "Who are you?"

"Doyle Hardy," he replied.

Instantly, Connie flew into a rage. "It's your fault," she screamed, attacking him with both fists, flailing her arms and screaming profanity at him.

Hardy stumbled backward, particularly when she hit his left shoulder still sore from Flem Thurman's shotgun blast.

"You're spreading lies, saying things that aren't true."

Hardy shoved her aside, then climbed astride the gray.

"He didn't kill his wife and son," she screamed pummeling his leg now that he was in the saddle, spooking the gray.

Hardy got the horse under control, spinning him in circles and calming him. "He killed them and might have killed you had you stayed with him."

"He loves me," she cried out, "planned to marry me." She charged for the gelding, but Hardy kept the horse circling her, just out of reach. "You're as mean as he said, beating him when he was a boy. He says you're the one that killed his wife and son, saying you'd forced yourself on her and that the boy was yours."

Biting his lip, Hardy wondered what kind of son he had really raised. Where did he go wrong? Maybe he should have been around at home more, but Tinnie made home so cold he never felt welcome, not even by his own son. How could he respond to this crazed girl? How could he counter Bud's lies? He couldn't. Connie would likely believe the lies forever.

Damn if Bud didn't have an oily way with women. He recalled a Fort Smith prostitute, named Nell Binder, who had fallen for him. Bud played her along, so the rumors had it, then took her for all the money she had saved from the business. The betrayed Nell Binder had left Fort Smith broke and heartbroken. Last Hardy had heard of her she was making the rounds of brothels in Choctaw Nation. Even after being swindled and dropped by him, she still cared for him.

The shame for Connie Boykin was that she would likely feel the same way about Bud Hardy, believing all his lies and thinking others had wronged him. Bud could mangle the truth and women.

Hardy was relieved to spot Connie's father approaching with a spare horse. Boykin reined up and jumped from his mount, running to his daughter and hugging her.

For a moment, Connie Boykin fought against her own father, then she fell apart into blubbering sobs.

"Bud shoved her off his horse," Hardy offered.

"The bastard," Boykin said.

At the word, Connie struck her father with her fist, but he grabbed it in his own powerful hand and squeezed it until she yelped in pain.

"He was a bad one," Boykin spat. "You're good to be shed of him, now and forever."

She tried but failed to push herself away from her father.

Boykin looked up to Hardy. "I'm obliged for what you've done, saving my daughter."

Hardy nodded. "Bud's a charmer, women believe his lies. His mother's been believing them for years."

"It true he's your son?"

This question kept coming up. Hardy wanted so badly to hide his paternity, but it was not in his constitution to lie about such matters. "Yes, I'm ashamed to say."

"I'm sorry, Deputy."

There was nothing else to be said. Hardy reined the gray around and started for Boggy Depot, easing from a walk to a trot and then a canter, the gray moving with long, even strides. The shadows were long now and the sky was starting to dim. Hardy knew Bud had a good start on him, but Bud lacked the trail smarts his father had honed over the years. Hardy would catch up tomorrow. He didn't want to get too anxious with darkness approaching. It would be better to catch Bud in the daylight than to risk an ambush in the night.

When Hardy saw a solitary rider round an approaching curve in the road, he pulled back softly on the reins and the gray slowed down. As the rider came within shouting distance, Hardy raised his hand for him to stop. "Deputy U.S. Marshal," Hardy called, "have you met any riders?"

The man straightened in his saddle, his hand falling stiffly to his side until he made out the badge on Hardy's chest.

"Seen any riders?"

"Three or four, one at a gallop."

"Was he riding a pinto?"

"Yeah, about a mile back down the road."

Hardy tipped his hat at the man. "Obliged." As Hardy kicked the gray's flank, the gelding galloped down the road.

Something, though, didn't ring just right. As much time as Bud had, he should be farther ahead on the trail, three, maybe four miles at the least. After all, Bud had ridden away from the Boykin place while Hardy had had to fetch his horse. Then Hardy lost additional time when he had tended the Boykin girl discarded like trash. Maybe Bud was trying to conserve his pinto's energy. On the other hand, if Bud were just a mile ahead, Hardy might be able to capture him before dark. Was that a prudent or just impatient option?

Alongside the road the trees stood as dark, silent sentries, ever vigilant for trespassers. The land was rumpled with hills and the gray followed the road around and between hills and occasionally up the hills. Overhead the sky was the last gold of dying light before it turned gray and then black.

Over the thump of the galloping hooves, he heard the caw of a crow and caught the movement of birds taking to wing from the bordering trees. He had about decided he should give up trying to catch Bud before dark when he turned a curve in the road, his gaze following the road to a gentle hill not a quarter of a mile away. Atop the hill, silhouetted against the sky, sat Bud on his pinto.

Hardy pulled back on his reins. This was odd. Bud was not the type to stand and fight unless it was from behind.

Bud lifted his arm and waved at Hardy, taunting him, daring him to approach.

Holding steady the pressure on the reins, Hardy brought the gray to a stop, then sat and stared.

Bud pulled a pistol from his holster.

Hardy saw a flash, then heard the report of the pistol. At this range, this display was nothing but a waste of ammunition.

Twice more Bud fired.

Hardy just stared. What was his intent?

Bud fired again.

Four bullets, thought Hardy, now wasted by Bud. And why wasn't Bud using his carbine?

Again Bud fired.

Perhaps Bud thought Hardy would chase head-long over the hill after him. Once Bud disappeared behind the rise, he could take a post beside the road and hope to knock Hardy out of the saddle as he raced by.

By Hardy's count, Bud fired the sixth bullet, then stuffed the empty gun back into his holster. Hardy knew Bud wore two side arms and had a carbine to boot on the side of his saddle. That's what made Hardy think this display was a trick.

Darkness was closing in and Hardy knew he had to make a decision. He nudged the gray forward into a trot.

Bud doffed his derby hat in what appeared to be a final taunt, then disappeared behind the hill.

Hardy advanced cautiously but quickly, reaching the hilltop and drawing up on the reins and looking at the road ahead. There was Bud not even a quarter of a mile away any more, his horse advancing at a walk as if he was on a Sunday afternoon excursion.

Hardy slapped his reins against the neck of his gray and charged for Bud. He was only halfway down the hill when he caught a flash from the side of the road and heard a gunshot. He twisted around in his saddle in time to see three men emerging from the darkness of the trees.

He recognized them as the LeHew brothers. Bud had led him into an ambush!

14

Up ahead Bud spun his pinto around and pulled his carbine from its scabbard.

Hardy saw Bud take aim. Hardy jerked the reins on the gray and the animal reared up, just as Bud fired. By the thud, Hardy knew the gelding had taken a bullet in the chest or belly.

Jerking his pistol from his belt, Hardy threw a wild shot at Bud, who slapped his pinto for the cover of the trees.

His gray fell back toward the ground, his front legs growing mushy. The horse stumbled forward.

Behind him, Hardy heard the pounding hooves of the LeHew brothers' horses. He turned his gray toward the cover of the woods. The animal stepped, then faltered.

Hardy twisted in the saddle and fired his pistol at the riders.

The LeHews answered with their own gunshots and Hardy felt the gray sag between his legs. He slapped the horse's rump and it made it to the edge of the woods, then collapsed.

"Get him," yelled Bud.

Hardy grabbed at the stock of his Winchester, but it slipped from his grasp as the gelding tumbled over. Jumping to clear the animal as it fell, Hardy hit the ground running and dove into the trees, just as a barrage of bullets whistled overhead.

He crawled on his belly deeper into the woods. He had his pistol, the bullets on his cartridge belt and nothing else except his wits. That would be enough to outsmart Bud, but Hardy wasn't so sure it would be enough against the three LeHews. Men who had spent seven years in prison on his account had had plenty of time to think about what they would do to the man who put them there. Now that they were just moments away from succeeding, they might not be deterred by anything.

"Where'd he go?" yelled Bud.

"Did we wing him?" came a voice Hardy recognized as Satch LeHew.

They pumped more bullets into the woods, none hitting close to Hardy. He heard horses gallop to where his gray had fallen.

The LeHews laughed. "He left his carbine," Satch announced. "Now, let's get the son of a bitch."

Hardy heard another horse approach.

"I'll tend the horses, boys, while you go kill him," called Bud.

Hardy cursed. His only chance was to lead the LeHews deeper into the woods, then circle back around them and try to capture a horse. But now, Bud had complicated that. Maybe Bud was shrewder at these things than Hardy had realized.

Glancing upward, Hardy noted dark sky. He at least had darkness for an ally. From the road, he heard the squeak of leather as men dismounted and retrieved their carbines.

Hardy lifted his pistol and aimed for the men as best he could see through the trees. The next time one of them spoke, Hardy would fire at the noise. He heard the sounds of bullets being levered into their carbines.

He aimed at the noise, then fired. The shot seemed to echo throughout the entire forest.

"Son of a bitch," shouted one of the LeHews.

"Let's go get him," shouted Satch.

Hardy started slipping through the woods, trying to make as much noise as possible without it becoming obvious that he was attempting to draw them away from their horses.

"We need torches or lamps," shouted one of the brothers.

"So he can see us?" answered Satch incredulously. "We'll find him in the dark."

"Just remember," said Bud, "you've got to bring me his badge and the warrant papers if you want your five hundred dollars."

"Just answer one question first," Satch demanded. "Did you really kill your woman and boy child?"

"What difference does it make?"

Satch laughed. "I just like to know what type of son of a bitch I'm working with."

Bud bragged, "I'm as mean as they come."

"Then," answered Satch, "you must've done it. Think you're smart enough to guard the horses and by all means don't let your pa's horse slip away." The three brothers laughed.

"Okay, boys, into the trees," commanded Satch LeHew.

To draw them deeper into the woods, Hardy fired another shot, then began to run as best he could through the dark, making all the noise he could.

"Spread out about ten yards apart and make sure we keep talking so we don't shoot each other," yelled Satch LeHew. "I hear him."

As Hardy advanced into the trees, he picked up pieces of dead wood and tossed them in different directions to fool the LeHews all the way.

"What was that?" called one LeHew when a big piece of wood landed with a crash.

The searcher fired at the noise.

Hardy saw the flash of gunfire, then aimed at the location and squeezed off a bullet. The gun flashed in the darkness. Hardy had forgotten how bright a flash gunfire created.

"Dammit," screamed another LeHew, "that was close."

"I seen the fire," called one, answering Hardy's shot with one of his own. The bullet whizzed dangerously close overhead. Hardy retreated deeper, figuring he was at least a hundred and maybe a hundred and fifty yards from the road.

Hardy then slid the pistol back in his holster. How many shots had he fired? Wasn't it three? He couldn't be sure in the darkness. He bent over and picked up anything that he could throw to confuse them of his whereabouts.

"He's over here," shouted Satch.

"No, closer to me," answered one of his brothers.

As Hardy rested to catch his breath, someone spooked a deer or another animal because the whole forest seemed to clatter. Quietly, Hardy circled wide of the noise, now trying to work his way back down to the horses. If he played it just right, he could slip up on Bud, capture him and start back to Fort Smith before the LeHew brothers ever figured out what might have happened.

Hardy halted at the sound of a twig snapping nearby. Was it someone or just his imagination? He wanted to move on, but forced himself to freeze. Just then one of the LeHew brothers passed by, not twenty feet away.

Hardy caught his breath and gave the outlaw plenty of time to keep going.

"You boys heard anything lately?" called the nearby LeHew.

"Nope," Satch replied.

"Dammit," called the near one. "Let's look a little more then circle back around and see if we can find the son of a bitch." He moved on, deeper into the woods.

Hardy let out a slow breath, then took small, careful steps back toward the road.

Now when he wanted to be quiet, every snapping twig beneath his foot seemed to echo through the woods.

With as much stealth as he could muster in the dark, Hardy slipped closer to the road. He heard the LeHew brothers calling to each other behind him. He grinned. He was halfway back to the road and they still hadn't figured out what had happened. Now, all Hardy had to do was slip up on Bud, disarm him and leave with the LeHews' horses. That wouldn't be too hard to do, Hardy figured. This had the potential of working out better than he thought.

Then Hardy froze at the shouts of the LeHews far behind him.

"He must've circled around us," Satch yelled. "He's going for the horses."

Damn! They had killed any chance of surprise. Behind him, Hardy could hear them firing off their guns, shouting and running through the woods as fast as they could.

Hardy moved quickly down to the road, trying to remember how many bullets he still had in his pistol. He thought he had fired three, but he wasn't certain any more. He couldn't load and weave through the trees at the same time so he would have to depend on however many bullets he had left in his Colt. He had a full cartridge belt and that would get him by. It would have to.

He made more noise than he liked, but there was no time for quiet, not with the LeHews charging at his back. Bud would know he was coming.

Up ahead he saw a break in the trees and knew he was approaching the road. His hand tightened around the pistol and he cocked the hammer, prepared to shoot. He heard horses stamping and blowing, but not in front of him, thirty yards to the left. That was okay. He could emerge from the woods here, follow the tree line to the horses and maybe have a better chance of surprising Bud.

"He's circled back for the horses," Satch kept shouting.

Hardy stopped a moment near the tree line, giving his breathing a chance to slow so Bud would not hear him heaving for air. Hardy could wait no longer, the noise of the LeHews kept drawing closer. He slipped out of the trees, squinting as if he could squeeze out enough light from the night to spot Bud.

Ahead Hardy could make out the dark profiles of the horses, tossing their heads and stamping at all the excitement. But for as much as he strained to see, he just saw three horses. Bud was gone.

Damn! Bud might be in the woods, waiting with his gun. Hardy could delay no longer. The LeHews were nearing. They were no more than fifty yards off, maybe closer. He was running out of time. He shoved his pistol into his holster and bolted for the horses, half expecting the woods to explode with gunfire at any moment. The horses jerked nervously at their reins. Already jumpy from the smell of Hardy's dead gray nearby, they were throwing their heads and whinnying with fright.

Hardy ran up to the horses and grabbed the reins of the nearest one. He tried to untie the leather strands, but the reins of all three were knotted around the same thin pine tree.

He heard a gunshot from the woods nearby and saw the flash. What was he to do? He fumbled with the reins again, the horses rearing as high as the reins would allow, the nearest one kicking at him with its hooves.

Hardy shoved his hand in his trousers and pulled out his pocketknife. Hurriedly, he unfolded the blade, grabbed the bridle strap of the nearest horse and worked his way down the reins, slicing through them at the tree. For a moment the horse fought him and tried to rear up and kick him, but Hardy held on. With knife in hand, Hardy managed to subdue the horse enough to climb aboard.

Now he heard the approaching LeHews and their mumbled curses as he fought to control his horse. He switched his knife and the reins to his left hand, then grabbed his pistol. He didn't have time to free the other two horses. Instead, he backed his mount toward them and cocked the hammer on his pistol. He managed to bring his skittish mount beside the closest horse. He shoved the pistol behind the horse's ear and fired. The horse collapsed on the ground. The remaining horse was terrified, kicking, stomping and tripping over the fallen horse at his feet.

A gunshot from the woods scorched the air over

Hardy's head. The LeHews were getting closer. Damn them! He had but seconds to kill the remaining horse. He cocked the hammer on his Colt again and pulled the trigger. The gun exploded. The horse quit fighting, but stood strangely still, like it had been stunned. Cocking the hammer and squeezing the trigger in one fluid motion, Hardy aimed as best the frightened horse beneath him would allow. The gun exploded and the second horse butted against the tree, then fell on its side.

One, then two LeHews burst from the woods.

Hardy ducked as they fired over his head. Shoving his pistol in his holster, he kicked his mount with his boots and slapped his free hand against its neck. The horse bolted down the road past the first two LeHews, but the third jumped out in the road and lunged for the reins, jerking them free. By reflex Hardy swatted at him with his left hand. Their arms met for a moment, then slid apart, the man screaming as Hardy bolted by. Only then did Hardy realize he still held the pocketknife and it had sliced across the man's arm.

The horse charged wildly down the road, the reins slapping against its legs as it ran, terrifying it even more. Hardy grabbed the saddle horn and just let the horse run free to put some distance between himself and the LeHews. Behind him he heard their gunshots and their curses as he galloped away in the darkness.

Using his leg against the back of the blade, he folded his pocketknife and clamped it between his teeth until he could get the horse under control. He took a deep breath and leaned forward, snagging the left rein and reeling it in, then switching hands on the saddle horn and grabbing the other rein with his right hand. Slowly he began to pull back on the reins, letting the horse ease off of its gallop. The mount's long strides shortened and its pace began to slow. Finally, the horse glided into a walk, allowing Hardy to return the knife to his trouser pocket.

As he settled back into the saddle, Hardy began to figure his losses. The gray was dead. He had had to abandon his saddle. The horse and saddle could ultimately be replaced but the loss of the carbine and the saddlebags was more serious. The carbine increased his defensive range and the saddlebags carried spare ammunition, plus the manacles he would need once he caught Bud.

Hardy shook his head at the thought of Bud. How typical of him to abandon the LeHews at the shootout. Bud didn't have the loyalty of a rattlesnake and he was a coward to boot. Of course, Hardy knew why Bud had left. He didn't have the five hundred dollars he had been promising people for his father's head. And now, Bud would not only have his father on his tail, but quite possibly the LeHew brothers as well. Hardy could only shake his head at how events sometimes made for strange alliances.

Now that Bud had abandoned the LeHews, Hardy figured his son was smart enough to keep on riding for fear the three brothers would come after him. Fear was a great motivator and Bud would likely ride like the devil all night and into the day, trying to put some distance between himself and the LeHews. Hardy figured Bud would ride hard for Boggy Depot, then lay over for a while. The last Hardy had heard, Boggy Depot was where Nell Binder now plied her trade. Bud had taken up with her after his marriage and had swindled her out of her savings, but she didn't care about that as much as keeping Bud. When he spurned her, she fell from the best brothel in Fort

Smith all the way down to the lowest shanties in Choctaw Nation.

While Bud might be riding like crazy through the night, Hardy knew he was safe for the night. It would be at least daylight before the LeHews could steal horses and maybe longer. By then, Hardy would have enough of a head start that he could likely apprehend Bud and start back to Fort Smith. He would have to be on the lookout for the LeHews, but it was nothing new. That was part of a deputy marshal's existence.

As Hardy rode along, he thought about Marshal Yoes's rules. He wondered how many he had broken. Since the LeHews weren't prisoners, he guessed it was okay to borrow one of their horses. Actually, he hadn't borrowed it, just traded his dead one with its saddle and saddlebags for a similarly outfitted one. Damn if he wasn't a good horse trader.

15

By morning and good light, Doyle Hardy stopped and dismounted, stretching his arms and his legs. He loaded his pistol and for the first time since climbing aboard the LeHew horse, Hardy took a look at the animal. It was a claybank, its jaundiced yellow coat about the ugliest Hardy had ever seen. Hardy unpinned his badge and slipped it in his coat pocket, not wanting to demean the dignity of the badge by being spotted on such an ugly horse. If the horse had anything it had to be heart and endurance because it sure wasn't looks. The horse was slightly pigeon-toed and had a head that was too big for its neck. Hardy figured he wouldn't have to worry about anyone stealing this homely animal.

Hardy yawned and estimated he had made ten to twelve miles during the night, putting himself about eight hours from Boggy Depot. He needed some sleep, but cursed that his stolen mount did not have a bedroll tied to the saddle. His bedroll was another loss he'd forgotten to add to the debit sheet of his encounter with the LeHews. To counter his drowsiness and the stiffness in his legs, Hardy led the claybank gelding down the road. Shortly, he reached a stream where he let the horse take its fill and where he splashed his face to cut the trail dust. The water was cool and he scooped handful after handful to his mouth. Hardy then moved off the road and out of sight of any passing riders. He found a patch of grass in the shade and tied his horse where it could graze while he napped. Hardy took off his coat and folded it in quarters for a pillow. Removing his hat as he lay down, he used it to cover his eyes as he rested his head on his makeshift pillow.

Hardy fell into a deep sleep that lasted for maybe four hours. He felt a gnawing in his stomach that finally awoke him. He had had nothing to eat since that twenty-five cent can of peaches late yesterday afternoon. Hardy stood up, tugging his hat over his head and unfolding his broadcloth coat. As he slipped his coat back on over his shoulders, he patted the inside pocket to make certain he hadn't lost the warrant for Bud Hardy. The paper was still there like the hunger in his stomach.

He walked over to his ugly horse, untied him and climbed into the saddle. It was a cheap saddle, not nearly as good as the one he had left behind on the gray. He led the horse to the road, then mounted and started for Boggy Depot. At a crossroads store a few miles down the road, he purchased some crackers and apples. He didn't request a receipt in this store, just retreated to his horse. As he turned the gelding toward Boggy Depot, he heard the proprietor snicker and call to a buddy to come look at Hardy's horse.

"I'd taken him for a deputy marshal," Hardy heard him say, "if he'd asked for a receipt or been riding a horse worth a damn."

At least the horse was good for something, if it threw people off the scent of his profession. Hardy ate the apples and crackers on the way to Boggy Depot. He met more horsemen and wagons in the afternoon than he had at any time since leaving Fort Smith. He realized the horse was so damn ugly that people were noticing it and then failing to notice the rider. Or maybe they were just too embarrassed for the rider to look him in the eye. Despite the horse's lack of appeal, he was a steady animal that made decent time and didn't resist Hardy's occasional urges to ride at a trot or canter.

It was a good hour after dark when Hardy approached Boggy Depot. He slumped low in the saddle to disguise his height as he rode into town. Seven roads converged at Boggy Depot, which had started out as a principal stage station on the Butterfield Mail and Stagecoach Line. Though the stage was gone, the town survived as a collection of houses and buildings facing a water well on a central square. Since the Missouri, Kansas and Texas Railroad came no closer than a dozen miles, Boggy Depot was in decline. A few people hung around, people who were too old or too stubborn to move. Hardy planned to call on one of the old-timers, a fellow named Noah Barnes who ran the hotel and eatery on the southeast corner of the square.

Hardy made the square, sighting nothing unusual, then pulled up in front of the Barnes Hotel, a two-story stone building that looked out across the town. After dismounting and tying the horse to the hitching post, he adjusted his gun belt and strode onto the wide porch, which was filled with a row of empty rocking chairs. He pushed open the door, a bell jingling atop it. The bell tinkled again as Hardy shut the door.

"We've no more rooms," Barnes said without looking up.

Hardy approached the desk, noting a man standing at the stairs, giving him the once over.

"I said we've no more rooms," Barnes said, glancing up at Hardy. A wave or surprise washed over his face. He started to say something, but Hardy shook his head, tipping him off not to indicate a familiarity that might be overheard.

"I'll sleep in your barn, if that's what it takes."

"Maybe we can figure something out," Barnes mused, "because I'd sure like to take your money."

The man at the stairs yawned, then began to climb the steps for his room. When he disappeared, Barnes smiled. "How are you, Doyle? Bad, I guess, from the news I hear about Bud?"

Hardy nodded. "It's not been the best of times for me."

"Is it true Bud killed his wife and boy?"

Again Hardy nodded. "Wish it weren't."

Barnes slowly shook his head, pinching the bridge of his nose and pursing his lips. "It don't make sense, does it?"

Hardy shrugged. "Nothing makes much sense any more. The boy's gone damn crazy, almost as crazy as his mama."

"Tinnie's still pestering you, is she? I used to think that about my wife till she up and died on me. I miss Mary Ann more than anything, Doyle." Barnes wiped at his eye, then glanced away for a moment.

There was nothing Hardy could say. If he ever felt as deeply for Tinnie, the emotion had been lost years ago.

Barnes pushed himself up from his desk. The years, magnified by the loss of his wife, showed in his lined face. Barnes looked old, though he was no more than a few years Hardy's senior. Maybe the loss of a loving woman aged a man more than living with a spiteful one. Then again, maybe other men thought Hardy was showing his age. Maybe that was why so many men were listening to Bud's five hundred dollar offer for his killing. In his younger days, Hardy would have thought they wanted to build a reputation. Now he wondered if they just thought his demise would be easy money.

Barnes moved around the desk, motioning for Hardy to follow him to a door under the stairway. "Our rooms are full up, but I've an extra bed in my compartment, if you don't mind sleeping in a daybed. It's comfortable, at least Mary Ann always thought so when we had to sleep apart in her final days."

Hardy, trying to remember the last time he had shared a bed with Tinnie, followed Barnes through the door and down the short hallway that led into Noah's bedroom. Beyond it was a small kitchen and parlor for the hotel proprietor.

"You wouldn't have any supper left over, would you?" Hardy asked. "All I've had since yesterday is some crackers and apples." Hardy followed Barnes into the kitchen, cluttered with dishes that needed washing and a pile of clothes that needed laundering.

"I ain't very good around the kitchen," Barnes answered. "Fact is, I ain't good at very much since Mary Ann died." Shaking his head, he stopped and pointed at a tin of biscuits and sausage atop the cold cookstove. "Take all the biscuits and meat you can stand. I've got to warn you, though, that I cooked them."

Hardy broke a biscuit in half and slid a patty of sausage between the pieces. He took a bite. The biscuit was hard and the sausage overcooked, but it was food nonetheless. He gobbled it down quickly, then took seconds.

Barnes pointed to the tiny parlor and the daybed against the far wall. "It's got a soft mattress, one that won't hurt your old bones. How's your rheumatism these days, Doyle?" Barnes sat down before the one clear spot on the table and shoved back some of the clutter for a spot where Hardy could pull up a chair.

Hardy polished off his second biscuit and sausage and reached for one more of each.

"Eat the whole damn plateful, Doyle."

Hardy took the tin and dropped it on the table in the spot Barnes had cleared. "My rheumatism acts up periodically, not enough to cripple me up, but enough to make me feel my age. Trailing Bud isn't making me any younger. It's a hard task for a man, trailing his own son." Hardy mulled over his fate before taking another sausage and biscuit and chewing absently.

Barnes rubbed his eyes, then his lined face. He licked his lips and cocked his head, just staring at Hardy.

Though Barnes said nothing, Hardy knew the hotel proprietor was bothered by something. Hardy also knew not to pry. Whatever it was, it was something Barnes had to bring up in his own way. They sat in silence for at least five minutes before Barnes spoke.

"You've been respected as an honest, decent man in all The Nations, tough but fair," Barnes started. "Bud's not that way."

"Maybe I didn't bring the boy up right, always being gone," Hardy started.

Barnes held up his hand. "Nobody blames you, Doyle, just that a lot of folks wonder if Bud is really your boy."

Hardy swallowed a half-chewed bite of biscuit and sausage, but it hung in his throat for a moment. It was a question he had never wanted to admit was a possibility. He just sat there, his eyes focusing on the tin plate of leftovers that he had made his supper.

"No offense, Doyle, but everyone knows Tinnie and that gambler . . ." Barnes's words trailed off into a silence of regret.

Hardy stared blankly ahead, his long silence uncomfortable.

"Doyle, I didn't mean to . . ."

Hardy shook his head and bit his lip.

Barnes grimaced.

"No matter what other folks say, the law says he's mine. I won't push my problems off on some roving gambler who happened to be in Fort Smith while I was in Indian Territory."

"Doyle," started Barnes but Hardy cut him off with a wave of his hand.

"No matter my differences with Tinnie, I won't go soiling her name now because her name is still half mine. And, the boy's name is all mine."

Barnes cleared his throat and took a deep breath as if apologizing for bringing the subject up. "I've never known a man that took an oath as seriously as you did, Doyle."

"If an oath don't mean something, then why swear to it."

"Why didn't you let somebody else track down Bud and stay in retirement? It wasn't your responsibility."

Hardy slowly shook his head. He realized that his hands were knotted so tightly into fists that his knuckles were white. "It is my responsibility, Noah. I raised a boy who killed his wife and my grandson, the last of the Hardy line, so I failed with Bud. Who else is to blame?"

Barnes stood up from the table, nervously pacing back and forth across the room. "What I'm trying to say, Doyle, is that nobody blames you. Nobody whose opinion and reputation you'd respect thinks you're at fault for how Bud turned out. Most think Bud was just bad seed. A few blame Tinnie, but nobody I've talked to blames you."

"It don't matter what other people think," Hardy responded, "when I blame myself."

Barnes coughed into his fist, then clenched his lips until he spoke. "Doyle, why don't you turn around, let one of the other deputies handle it."

"Can't do it, Noah. Bud's put a five hundred dollar price on my head. Every idiot with a gun between the Arkansas and the Red rivers will be looking for me to collect on that money. Until Bud's captured . . . ," Hardy paused, ". . . or killed, my life's in danger because of him."

Turning away from the table, Barnes released a long, steady breath that whistled. "I was afraid you would say that."

"Why, has Bud been seen in town?"

The hotel proprietor nodded.

"Consorting with a whore named Nell Binder?"

Noah Barnes spun around. "How'd you know?"

Hardy stood slowly up from the table. "Bud's always run to women when he was in trouble. When he was a kid, I couldn't whip him when he needed it without him running to Tinnie. She'd defend him, saying he couldn't do wrong or didn't mean any harm. Women have always trusted him and he's always used them."

Barnes pinched the bridge of his nose. "I can

understand that, but this Nell Binder, how'd you know her name?"

"Noah, I chased outlaws for some thirty years. I know about the bad side of life, the bad people. You know what happened to Nell Binder? Bud took up with her in Fort Smith after he got married. He swindled her out of her savings, she trying to make something respectable of herself and him taking not only her money but her hope as well away from her. After he got her money, he discarded her like trash. And you know what? She begged him to take her back, then fell to pieces when he didn't."

Shaking his head, Barnes paced back and forth between the table and the cold cookstove. "I didn't know."

"It wasn't something I was prone to tell people. Do you know where Nell Binder plies her trade?"

Barnes delayed answering.

"Do you?"

Now Barnes nodded. "But I hate to tell you."

"I can find him, Noah."

"I don't want to be a party to you killing your son, Doyle, that's all."

Hardy shook his head. "Bud's a coward. He won't let himself get killed. He'd shoot me in the back, but he wouldn't face me in a fair fight. Once I get the drop on him, he'll give up."

"What if he doesn't?"

"I'll take him, one way or the other."

Barnes dropped his head. "It'd be a heavy burden to carry, killing your own son, Doyle, even if he isn't really yours."

"No harder burden than knowing he killed my daughter-in-law and only grandson. The law still says he's mine."

"You're the stubbornest man I've ever seen, Doyle."

Hardy shrugged, then yawned. "It's getting bedtime and I'll need to be up early to catch Bud."

"Or shoot him." Barnes sighed.

"Or shoot him," Hardy repeated.

Barnes pointed to the parlor and the daybed. "There's your roost for the night. Need me to stable your horse for you?"

Hardy shook his head. "Leave it hitched out front. As ugly as he is, nobody'd steal him except in the dark. If they do, I want to be gone by dawn so they can't return him."

16

When he awoke, Hardy realized something was amiss. The tiny parlor was swathed in a gentle morning light. He had overslept, but the rest on a soft mattress had done him good. For the first time in days, Hardy felt he was starting out fully rested. As he began to stir, he heard Noah Barnes stumble through the kitchen and out the back door to get his morning relief.

Hardy pushed himself up from the bed, then stretched and dressed, joining Barnes at the outhouse. As Barnes emerged, Hardy nodded his greeting and slipped inside to attend to his business. When he came out, Barnes stood waiting.

"You must be getting old, Doyle. You either overslept or told me a lie last night about being up at dawn."

"You've got a good mattress there."

"I guess so, seeing as how you snored like a locomotive all night."

Hardy glanced over his shoulder as they started back for the hotel. "Does Nell Binder have an outhouse?"

Barnes wrinkled his nose. "What?"

"Does Nell Binder have an outhouse behind her place?"

"Don't most folks? I don't know. What's it matter?"

"Just trying to figure a way to catch Bud with no chance of him getting hurt."

At the hotel, they stepped back into the kitchen, Barnes offering to fix a little breakfast. Hardy shook his head. "I need you to take me to Nell's so I can get this dance over with."

Hardy gathered his hat, strapped on his gun belt, checked the load in his pistol and emerged with Barnes out the back.

"Give me a minute to saddle my horse," Barnes said, trotting to the small barn beyond the outhouse.

Hardy marched around to the front of the hotel to find his pigeon-toed mount, its head hanging low. The horse looked at him without lifting his head, then swished his tail. Hardy felt the horse was trying to shame him for not stabling him overnight. Reaching the gelding, Hardy untied the reins and scratched him behind the ears. The horse tossed its head, then brushed against Hardy, pushing him aside. Hardy led the horse away from the hitching rail, then mounted, letting the animal trot around in a tight circle to work off some of its restlessness. Shortly Barnes, astride a red mare, rode around the hotel and started across the square. Hardy fell in behind him. They rode past a half dozen buildings to a fork in the road. Barnes turned his mare south onto the Tishomingo Road for a quarter of a mile, then pointed to a small cabin hidden among the trees some thirty yards off the trail.

"That's Nell's place. Her and another girl are working out of the shack."

The first thing Hardy noticed about the place was Bud's horse hitched out front where he had left it all night. Hardy shook his head. A man should take better care of his horse than that. Then Hardy remembered leaving the claybank outside the hotel for the night. He shook his head.

Hardy studied the dilapidated cabin. It was a damn shame what Bud had driven Nell Binder to. At least back in Fort Smith, the house she had worked had gaslights, indoor plumbing and clean sheets. Except for vermin, this crib exceeded the Fort Smith brothel at nothing.

Barnes coughed into his fist. "I'm heading back, Doyle. I don't want to be here for the finish."

"Neither do I," Hardy admitted.

"There's still time to back out, let someone else do it."

Hardy shook his head. "Nope, I took an oath."

"I hope that oath don't get you or Bud killed today."

Pulling back his broadcloth coat, Hardy hooked it behind the butt of his Colt revolver. "That's up to him."

Barnes reined his horse around toward Boggy Depot.

"One thing more, Noah," Hardy asked. "When the store opens up, buy me some leather bootlaces and thirty-five feet of good rope."

"Damn, Doyle, you're not gonna to hang him yourself, are you?"

"I lost my manacles in an ambush, Noah, and I'll need something to tie him up. Now get moving before Bud comes out and spots us."

Without another word, Barnes kicked the mare and she darted back down the road to Boggy Depot. Hardy wished Barnes hadn't left at a canter because of the noise. Hardy shrugged and rode on, then turned off into the woods, dismounted and tied his horse. Overhead the sky had assumed the color of day. He slipped through the woods toward the crib, approaching it from its windowless side. Out back, he saw an outhouse. Hardy thought he could wait for Bud to heed nature's call, then surprise him. But what if Bud had already answered his morning call?

Just then, the outhouse door swung open and Bud emerged, holding his head and screening his eyes from the soft glow of morning light. He was fully dressed, except for his gun belt. Too much liquor last night, Hardy figured. Bud disappeared back inside the cabin.

The woods could provide cover for Hardy all but the last fifty feet of the way to the crib. Hardy figured to make a dash for the blind side of the cabin. What he would do when he got there, he still wasn't certain. Hardy slipped from the trees, crouched low over the ground and moved quickly toward the house. He made it easily, then held his breath so he could hear and not be heard. Bud's pinto stomped and fidgeted for a moment.

From inside, Hardy heard Bud say something followed by a woman's giggle. What women saw in Bud, Hardy could only guess. It wasn't integrity and it wasn't loyalty, he thought as he weighed his options. He must either wait Bud out or draw him out without alerting him why.

A loud giggle came from inside, then Bud cursed. "Get up and fix me some breakfast."

The woman's giggle turned to a hurt whimper. "Why do you treat me this way?" asked the woman.

"You're nothing but a whore," Bud shouted.

Hardy shook his head. Where had he gone wrong with his son? Bud's pinto whinnied, giving Hardy an idea. He pulled his knife from his britches and opened the blade. Crouching below the front cabin windows he slid over to the hitching rail and cut the horse's reins. Then he slipped back from the hitching post to the corner of the house. After closing his knife and slipping it back into his pocket, Hardy took off his hat and flung it at the pinto. Instantly, Hardy whipped his Colt from its holster.

The hat flew into the pinto's neck, scaring the gelding. It neighed, jerked its head and bolted toward Boggy Depot, its hooves pounding against the hard-packed trail.

"What the hell?" Bud shouted from inside.

The door swung open and Bud jumped out, his gaze following the direction of the retreating pinto. "Dammit to hell," he cursed, shoving his hands on his hips just above the twin pistols he was now wearing.

Instantly, Hardy leaped behind him and shoved his gun in his back. "Morning, Bud," he whispered through tight lips, "there's a .45 in your back just waiting to send you to Hell if you try anything."

Bud gulped.

With his free left hand, Hardy slipped the left pistol out of Bud's holster and shoved it in his own belt. Carefully he moved until he could reach the right pistol. He removed it and slid it in his belt as well.

"Damn you," Bud spat out.

As Hardy pulled Bud back to the windowless side of the cabin, he saw two women stride out of the crib.

One carried a derringer and the other a small revolver. The one with the small revolver was Nell Binder. Hardy barely recognized her, she had aged so. The chipped front tooth was the only thing that confirmed it was her.

"You ladies drop your guns before somebody gets hurt."

Nell Binder strode brazenly forward, closing the top of her nightgown with one hand and waving the pistol with her other. When she started to speak, her words were slightly slurred and incoherent. "You already hurt him enough, killing his wife and son. And then blaming it on him so you'd have an excuse to kill him. I love him if she never did, even though he had a son by her." Hardy realized she was drunk. Tripping on her gown, she stumbled forward then fell, the gun sliding toward Bud.

Bud lunged for the gun and wrapped his fingers around it just as Hardy stomped on it with his boot. Bud screamed, grabbed his wrist and rolled over.

Hardy squatted and retrieved the revolver, keeping his gun on the second prostitute.

She raised her hands. "Don't shoot."

"Drop it," he ordered.

The derringer fell from her hand to the ground.

Beside Bud on the ground, Nell Binder took to sobbing. "Don't take him away, please. I love him, I'll take care of him." She grabbed for Hardy's leg as she babbled her devotion to Bud.

Hardy stepped away from her grasp, then grabbed Bud by the arm and jerked him off the ground.

Bud cursed him with language so foul that Hardy struck him across the cheek with the gun barrel. Bud staggered for a moment, his brown eyes focusing all the hate they could muster on his father.

"Don't use that language in front of ladies."

"They ain't ladies," Bud answered.

"That's not for you to say. You didn't learn any of the manners I taught you as a kid."

Bud thrust his chin forward. "Put down the gun, old man, and I'll take you on with my fists."

Hardy shoved Bud backward, then bent over and picked up the hat he had thrown at the pinto. "It's time we start back for Fort Smith and a trial."

As Hardy put on the hat, Bud began to laugh crazily. "You'll never get me back to Fort Smith. I've promised five hundred dollars to any man who'll kill you. They'll be fighting to get their hands on you."

"You don't have five hundred dollars, Bud."

He laughed again. "Yeah, but they don't know it."

Hardy tossed Nell Binder's small revolver on the cabin roof, then picked up the derringer and did the same thing with it. He pushed Bud toward his clay-bank hidden among the trees.

"We'll get my mount then retrieve yours. You can either cooperate and walk, Bud, or I'll give you a headache unlike any you've ever had."

For the first time, Bud went along with his father's orders, but Hardy knew it was only because he was saving his strength for later down the trail.

They reached Hardy's horse quickly and the deputy mounted.

Bud stared as Hardy got control of the horse. "That's Satch LeHew's horse, isn't it?"

"Not any more."

"What happened to them?"

"Last I saw they were looking for their horses. They'll have some questions to ask you about abandoning their horses and them."

Bud laughed. "Why, you got the jump on me and

forced me to ride away with you, don't you remember?"

Hardy shook his head. "Why do you think you can lie your way out of everything, Bud?"

"Who are the LeHews going to believe, you or me?"

"How are you going to lie your way out of killing your own wife and son?"

"I didn't kill them," he insisted, folding his arms across his chest.

"Then how do you explain this?" Hardy rose in his saddle and shoved his hand in his pants pocket. He pulled out a necklace with a spent .45-caliber hull for a pendant. "I found this in Molina's hand, Bud." Hardy held the necklace up between his fingers. "I pried this from her stiff fingers, Bud. Whose was it? Who was so proud of killing his first man and getting away with it that he wore the spent hull around his neck?"

Hardy saw Bud's shoulders sag. "I lost the necklace."

"Damn right you did, in the attack on Molina and Daniel."

"No, no," Bud shouted, "before that."

"Tell it to Judge Parker, Bud. You'll have plenty of time to make up your story before we get back to Fort Smith."

"Then let's get going instead of standing here yapping." Bud spun around and marched back toward the cabin and his horse which was grazing just at the far edge of the trees.

Wadding the necklace in his fist, Hardy shoved it back in his pants pocket. Hardy gave his horse loose rein, then nudged the animal when Bud began to pick up his pace. Hardy saw the reason why Bud was suddenly interested in getting to his pinto—his carbine. Hardy slapped the reins against his horse's neck and the animal bolted by Bud and quickly was beside the pinto.

Leaning over in the saddle but watching Bud out of the corner of his eye, Hardy jerked the .44-40 saddle gun free and slid it in the empty scabbard beneath his own saddle. Bud's carbine stock was as gaudy as a prostitute in church, Bud having nailed brass tacks to the wood to draw more attention to himself. Hardy shook his head. Were Bud as decent as he was vain, he'd be a church deacon. Hardy caught the shortened reins of the pinto and led it back to Bud.

"Mount up and don't try anything."

Bud spat at the hooves of his father's horse. "It's a long way to Fort Smith."

Hardy tapped his coat at the breast. "The warrant for your arrest is here. If there's any problem, I can kill you and drag your carcass back. There won't be any questions asked."

"You may have a warrant but I don't see any badge." Bud climbed begrudgingly into the saddle.

"My badge is in my pocket."

"Why don't you pin it on your chest so folks'll know what a big man you are." Then he laughed as he settled into his leather seat. "And so my friends will have a good target."

Hardy motioned for his son to pass.

Bud smirked as he rode by. "It's a long way to Fort Smith."

"And it's a short way to Hell if you try anything, Bud."

Bud laughed as he rode past the two prostitutes. They stood in the cabin doorway, holding each other and crying.

"They like me," Bud taunted. "That's more than I can say about how mama feels about you." He laughed.

Hardy felt the anger rising in him. He knew Bud was playing with his nerves. He knew it would be a longer ride for him back to Fort Smith than for Bud. Hardy would have to be on alert every minute, while Bud could pick and choose his time of attack.

"Yep, your own wife don't even like you," Bud called out as they hit the road back to Boggy Depot.

"Once she did," Hardy said quietly.

As Hardy followed Bud toward the square, he reached into his pocket and pulled out his badge. Maybe it was time to pin the metal star on his chest so everyone would know what was going on.

Up ahead in town, men and a few women walked the street, stopping to stare as Hardy and Bud rode by. Bud put on a show, bowing at the waist and shouting to every man with a gun.

"Five hundred dollars to any man—or woman— who kills the deputy behind me. It's easy money. He's old and slow."

One of the spectators pointed at Hardy and took off his hat.

"Damn if that ain't Doyle Hardy, the best damn deputy that ever rode Choctaw Nation or anywhere else."

"Five hundred to kill him," Bud shouted almost maniacally.

Hardy looked from man to man, most were taking off their hats and tipping them to him. Suddenly, someone began to clap and then everyone applauded as he rode past.

Doyle Hardy tipped his hat to the men and

women of Boggy Depot. It gave him an odd feeling, this show of appreciation. He was embarrassed by it, yet proud of its spontaneity and its deflating impact on Bud.

Bud Hardy slumped in the saddle and shook his head.

"Did decent folks ever clap for you, Bud, or just whores?"

Bud ignored the question.

"Head for the hotel," Hardy ordered and, to his surprise, Bud obeyed.

Father and son reined up at the hotel.

"Noah Barnes," yelled Hardy.

In a moment the hotel proprietor barged out the door, carrying a coil of rope and a handful of leather laces. "I'm glad you didn't have to hurt him, Doyle."

Bud stared sullenly ahead as folks gathered around the horses.

"Get down, Bud," Hardy commanded as he climbed out of his own saddle, "and turn around facing your saddle."

Again Bud obeyed and Hardy searched him, finding a knife and scabbard tucked in the back of his britches. The feel of the knife in his hands sent a chill up his spine. This was the steel that had killed Molina and Daniel. He tucked the knife in his own boot and continued the search, finding a derringer in Bud's pocket and a flask of whiskey in his hand-stitched boot. Doyle handed Barnes the derringer, then clamped his teeth around the whiskey cork and jerked it from the flask. He dumped the whiskey on the dirt at Bud's feet, the liquor splattering the fancy leather work of his boots.

When he was confident that Bud had no other hidden weapons or contraband upon him, Hardy took the leather laces from Barnes and tied his wrists together, jerking the leather strands tight, hoping to make Bud squeal in pain in front of the others, but his son gritted his teeth without making a noise.

Barnes used another leather thong to tie the coiled rope over Hardy's saddle horn, then scampered back into the hotel and returned in a moment with a bundle of food tied in a dish towel. "It's fresh biscuits and sausage with a bunch of dried apples."

"Obliged, Noah," Hardy said. He pulled Bud's ivory-handled pistols from his britches and handed them to Barnes. "Sell them for what you can get to cover the cost of the rope and keep the difference. Bud won't be needing them any more."

"Son of a bitch," growled Bud.

"Get in the saddle," Hardy commanded Bud.

His son held up his bound hands. "With this?"

"Loop them over the saddle horn and mount yourself."

Bud grumbled, but after two tries made it into the saddle.

Hardy handed him the reins and issued a warning. "Don't try anything you'll regret."

"You're looking for an excuse to kill me, aren't you." Bud surveyed the spectators. "He killed my wife and boy and now's trying to blame it on me."

A wiry man stepped beside Bud and shook a skinny finger at his nose. "Doyle Hardy never did nothing but decent things for decent people around here. Scream till you don't have a voice and nobody'll believe you even then."

Bud dropped his head and seemed to stare at his bound hands resting on the saddle horn.

Hardy climbed atop his homely horse. "Give us room to pass," he called and a path opened through the crowd. Hardy tipped his hat. "Thank you," he said and the decent folk applauded again. He turned to Barnes. "I'm sorry about Mary Ann."

Barnes bit his lip. "I'm sorry for you. A lot of decent folks around here still don't believe he's your boy."

Hardy turned his horse and his son toward Fort Smith.

17

Bud rode silently, his eyes fixed on the road ahead. When he looked to the side, it was always the side opposite where Doyle Hardy rode. Hardy stayed either behind him or to his right where Bud could not make a lunge for the pistol Hardy carried high on his right hip.

They went past noon without so much as a word and that was fine with Hardy. He kept having this sensation, that he was being followed. Several times, he glanced back over his shoulder thinking he would see someone, but all he saw was empty road. Occasionally they met a rider or a wagon, but mostly it was just the two of them .

An hour or more after high sun, Bud spoke. "We gonna eat?"

"In a bit."

They rode a couple of miles more.

"I didn't have breakfast, you arresting me before the girls could fix my meal."

Hardy nodded. "I didn't have breakfast either."

Bud grumbled. "That your plan, to starve me to death."

"Is it your plan to pester me to death?"

Wordlessly, they traveled another hour and all the time Hardy wondered if he was being followed and, if so, how closely. Finally, around a bend in the road, he motioned for Bud to enter the woods and he followed him.

"It's about time we ate," Bud said.

"Shut up," Hardy answered, pulling his gun and waiting, the minutes dragging by like hours. He was about to give up when he thought he heard the soft fall of a horse approaching at a walk.

At this same moment, Bud seemed to realize what Hardy was doing. "Run," Bud screamed, "he's waiting to ambush you. Run, dammit, run."

Hardy drew back his pistol to strike Bud across the side of the face, then heard the sound of galloping hooves retreating back up the road. He raced his horse out of the trees and around the curve in time to see a man on a black horse disappearing over the hill.

Fearing Bud might try to escape, Hardy spun his mount around and galloped back to where he had left his prisoner. Bud, still having trouble guiding his horse with his hands tied, was just emerging from the woods, a smile upon his face. "Must be one of my friends coming to rescue me."

"He won't need to rescue you if you do that again."

"Big talk."

Hardy pointed down the road to Fort Smith. "Start riding."

Bud laughed as he resumed his journey to court. Hardy didn't push the horses, figuring to take it slow in case they needed to make a run for safety. At the pace they were traveling, they would have four days and nights on the trail.

Just before the sun slipped behind the trees, they crossed a stream where Hardy let the horses water and blow. Then he helped Bud from the saddle so he could drink his fill of water. Only when the horses and his prisoner were done did he dismount and take water for himself.

After helping Bud back in the saddle, Hardy pointed downstream. "Ride that direction and stay in the water."

Bud grumbled about being hungry, but followed orders. Hardy tailed him. If someone were following, this might throw them for a bit. An experienced tracker wouldn't have much trouble figuring out what had happened, but Hardy doubted the man on their tail had any tracking skills.

About a half mile downstream, they came to a flat-topped, rock-rimmed rise that the stream skirted. Hardy grabbed the reins from Bud and led him up the rise. There they dismounted.

Hardy aimed his finger at a big rock. "Go sit over there with your back against it."

"Are we gonna eat?"

Ignoring Bud, Hardy hobbled the horses and unsaddled them. He tossed Bud's saddle toward him, then went through his saddlebags, looking for weapons. Though he found no weapons, he uncovered another flask of whiskey and dashed it against the rocks.

He unrolled Bud's bedroll and found nothing out of the ordinary except a tintype of his mother. Hardy smiled. It was taken before Bud was born and before Boone Dillon, when Tinnie was still the woman he had married, not some embittered shrew who had crawled into her own world. He wished she had never changed. Then Hardy wondered if Bud had a photograph of his own wife and son.

"I found the tintype of your mama," he said.

"Leave it alone."

"You got a photograph of Molina and Daniel? Photographs are cheaper than the tintypes we had to get made."

"I never had the money."

"The hell you didn't, Bud. You swindled all the money that Nell Binder had saved by letting men root over her." Hardy shoved the tintype in his coat pocket.

"She gave me that money."

Hardy spat with disgust and wadded Bud's bedroll up and threw it at him. Bud cursed as it landed at his feet.

"Watch your language or I'll use your bedroll. I lost mine to the LeHew brothers." For a pillow Hardy propped his saddle against a rock and for a bedroll he had only the saddle blanket. At least he had some supper. He grabbed the food bundle Noah Barnes had provided and untied the twine around the cloth's neck. He extracted a single biscuit and sausage, tossing them at Bud.

"There's your supper."

Bud snatched at them in the air, but missed and scrambled to the ground to retrieve the food. "That's all?"

"For tonight and it's more than I'm having." A hungry stomach kept a man on edge and Hardy wanted to be alert tonight in case Bud tried something. "Eat it slowly and it'll last longer."

Bud didn't listen, gobbling the sausage and biscuit greedily in a couple of bites.

When he was done, Hardy ordered him to take off his boots. Bud fought them off his feet, then Hardy took another of the leather laces and tied it around Bud's ankles.

"I ain't going anywhere." Bud grinned.

"That's the idea," Hardy answered.

Bud dragged his saddle where he could use it as a pillow, then smoothed out his bedroll and crawled in.

Hardy carried Bud's boots to his own saddle, then slid Bud's carbine under the saddle so there was no chance Bud could get to it. Hardy leaned his shoulders and head against the saddle and watched night creep across the sky.

When it was dark, Hardy asked a question he had to have answered. "Why'd you do it?"

"I don't have to answer that."

Hardy nodded in the dark. "That's right, but if you want another sausage and biscuit or anything else to eat between here and Fort Smith, you better."

There was a long silence. "I'd had too much to drink." He paused as if ashamed to admit more. "I thought she was seeing another man."

The answer struck Hardy like a runaway locomotive. He'd often wondered how well Tinnie had known Boone Dillon. "Molina wasn't that type. Anyway, you'd been consorting with other women, evil women."

"That's what they're there for."

"Didn't you take a marriage oath?"

"Oaths don't mean nothing. They're for fools."

Hardy could only shake his head.

"But why the boy, too?"

"I thought he was her bastard offspring."

Hardy clenched his teeth. He had begun to wonder that very thing about Bud Hardy. Was Bud out of the union of Tinnie Hardy and Boone Dillon? "I've thought the same thing about you, Bud."

Bud shot up from his bedroll and spat at Hardy. "Damn you! You're my pa whether you want to admit it or not. And mama isn't that kind of woman. Take it back or I'll kill you, you bastard." He scrambled to get up, but forgot about the laces on his feet until he fell flat on his face. "You bastard," he shouted, spitting the dirt from his mouth.

"You ever hear of a man named Dillon?"

"You bastard," he screamed.

"Boone Dillon?"

Bud fell suddenly quiet.

In the darkness Hardy could not see the expression on Bud's face. "Boone Dillon was his name. I never saw him. I was in The Nations at the time. I just heard what other people said. Boone Dillon. You ever heard of him?"

When Bud answered, his voice was soft. "I never heard of any Dillon, but when I was little mama used to tell me stories of a man named Boone. She always called him 'the frontier prince Boone' and made up stories of his adventures all over Indian Territory and the west. She'd tell me these stories when you were in The Nations and I used to think it was you she was talking about, but she insisted it wasn't. She said you could never be as adventurous and handsome as the frontier prince Boone. She threatened never to tell me any more stories of him if I ever told you about him. I always wanted to, but sometimes I thought she didn't want me to have anything to do with you. It was almost like she believed the frontier prince Boone would one day come for her."

Hardy swallowed hard. "Your mama never was the same after Boone Dillon."

"I came to believe the frontier prince Boone was Daniel Boone." His voice wavered. "That's why I named my boy 'Daniel.' And now, I've kilt him. I didn't meant to. It just happened."

Twisting uncomfortably, Hardy grunted. "It didn't just happen, Bud. Your mama turned you against me, against everything I stood for. I was a lawman so she was against rules for you. She saw that you got out of the whippings you deserved."

"Dammit, you weren't there when I was growing up."

Hardy spat. "I felt more welcome out here in The Nations than I did at home."

"Then why'd you retire?"

"I figured one day I'd have to arrest you if I stayed with the Marshal's office. In spite of our disagreements, I didn't want that. I always considered you my son."

Bud laughed. "Then why'd you come after me?"

"Because you killed kin. You turned against me like your mama had years ago. Molina and Daniel, my only grandson, were all the folks I had left."

"How do you know Daniel was your grandson?"

"How do I know you're my son, Bud?"

"You bastard," Bud shouted. "Mama wasn't that way."

Hardy locked his hands beneath his neck and stared up at the stars slowly emerging from the dark curtain of night. Bud never knew his mama when she was the woman Hardy married.

"You bastard," Bud repeated, his voice suddenly lower and more menacing. "I'll kill you."

Hardy bit his lip. Had Tinnie turned the boy against him? Or did Bud have Boone Dillon's restless, irresponsible blood coursing through his veins? With more direction and discipline than Tinnie would allow, would Bud have turned out decently like Emma Sims's boys?

"I'll kill you before we get to Fort Smith," Bud growled.

"I figure you'll try once, but you'll get but one chance, Bud, so make the best of it."

"You'd love to kill me, get back at mama, wouldn't you?"

"My son, if I ever had one, died long ago. I don't care to kill you, but I will if I have to. What I'd like to do is whip you like I should've done years ago. Maybe if I had, Molina and Daniel would still be alive. "

"You bastard."

"Shut up and go to sleep, Bud. You've still got a long ride ahead of you." Hardy turned over. He pondered whether he should tie Bud to a tree. After all, that's why he had bought the rope; even so, it was difficult to treat Bud as hard as he deserved. Maybe Bud was his son, maybe he wasn't, but Hardy had always considered him his boy and the law made him so.

So many questions, so many doubts came to Hardy's mind that he couldn't go to sleep. The doubts gnawed at his brain like the hunger at his stomach. Sleep avoided him and gradually Bud's low snoring seemed to taunt him for his insomnia. When sleep did come, it came hard upon him, knocking him dangerously out. He dreamed of Tinnie and how she had been before Boone Dillon. He dreamed of being in her arms and enjoying her as a man can enjoy a woman. And then, their marital bliss was interrupted by someone who stayed in the shadows of Hardy's dream. He thought he saw Boone Dillon.

And then Hardy jolted awake with a start.

From nowhere something crashed into his stomach.

Hardy sat up, catching his breath.

Bud? What was Bud doing?

Hardy heard a noise behind him, then a laugh. It was Bud.

Before he could turn around or grab his gun, Hardy felt a leather strap jerked over his forehead, sliding down his nose and moving under his chin to his neck. He reached for the leather thong, grabbing it as it began to tighten around his neck.

Bud laughed. "Now you'll die, you bastard."

Hardy felt his head jerked backward as the thong bit into the flesh of his neck.

Bud was trying to strangle him.

18

His lungs burned for want of air and Bud's hot, labored breath at his ear taunted him as he kicked and flailed at the ground. His right hand was trapped between the thong and his neck. He reached with his left hand for the gun on his right hip and managed to pull it from his holster, but the gun slipped from his grasp as Bud tightened his hold around Hardy's neck.

"Die, you bastard, die!" Bud kept repeating.

Hardy was growing weaker by the second. He pulled against the thong with his hand and tried to jerk Bud forward but he lacked the leverage. He bent his legs and powered his whole body back into Bud, who stumbled backward over the saddle that had been his pillow.

Cursing, Bud crashed into the rock, his head snapping, his hands loosening for a moment.

Hardy jerked at the thong, giving himself slack for air and gasping for breath as he tried to lift the thong from his neck.

Bud bucked and tried to toss Hardy aside. He failed and cursed.

Hardy lifted his left arm and brought it crashing into Bud's ribs. Bud cried out in pain just long enough for Hardy to throw Bud's hands up and to slip from under the leather thong.

Bud cursed again, but his epithet rang of fear instead of triumph.

Hardy rolled over, holding Bud to the ground. Simultaneously, he lifted his fist and his knee. He pounded Bud's cheek with his fist and threw his knee into Bud's groin. Bud cried out in pain, then convulsed in agony, throwing Hardy aside as he grasped at his groin.

While Bud trembled with pain, Hardy scrambled on his hands and knees to find his pistol. He shoved it under Bud's ear. "I should kill you for that." With the back of his left hand Hardy slapped him across the face. "You had your chance, Bud, and you failed. Killing me's not as easy as killing your wife and son." He slapped him again.

Bud lifted his hand to defend himself as Hardy shoved the pistol against his temple. Bud pushed it away.

Hardy pinned Bud's arms, straddled him and lifted his knee again, aiming for Bud's groin.

"Don't," Bud screamed, "not there."

"Why not, dammit?" Hardy screamed. "You won't be needing your dinger in prison because there ain't women there. And I'm gonna get you to prison."

Bud's arms dropped to his side and he went limp with surrender.

Hardy still huffed for breath. "No breakfast for you."

Bud groaned, then rolled over onto his hands and knees. Hardy could just make him out in the darkness. At that moment Hardy realized Bud was trying to fish his carbine from under Hardy's saddle.

"Dammit, Bud, I'm tired of fooling with you."
Hardy lifted his gun, then crashed the barrel against
the side of Bud's head. Bud tumbled to the ground in
a clump.

Hardy leaned back against the rock and began the
wait for dawn. He dozed off lightly, gun in hand.
When sunrise came as a glow behind the trees, he
stood up, reholstered his pistol and rubbed his tender
neck which was especially raw where the leather had
bitten into the flesh. The furrow in his neck was sticky
with clotted blood.

Hardy knew he should have treated Bud no differ-
ently from any other prisoner because all are desperate
men. He had given Bud the benefit of the doubt. Bud
would not get a second chance. Hardy toed at Bud
with his boot, drawing a groggy groan. Certain that
Bud wouldn't be going anywhere very fast if he did
get up, Hardy saddled the claybank and slid the carbine in place. Next he attended to Bud's pinto. When
he was done with that, he picked up the food bundle
Noah Barnes had provided and took out a stale
sausage and biscuit, eating the meager breakfast
slowly to fool himself it was more than it actually was.
His stomach was not fooled and growled for more.

When he was done, he rolled Bud over onto his
back and saw that Bud's hands were still tied together,
but not as Hardy had tied them. Apparently, Bud had
undone the leather thong, then retied it around each
wrist to use as a garrote. Hardy unknotted the strands,
then turned Bud over on his stomach and pulled his
arms behind his back, tightly tying his wrists together.
Bud moaned as Hardy cinched the leather. Bud had
untied his legs as well, but that no longer mattered.
Hardy wouldn't tie Bud's legs again.

Bad thing about Bud's attack and the subsequent

blow to his groin was that Bud would sit gingerly in the saddle, slowing the return to Fort Smith.

Hardy rolled Bud over on his side and noticed for the first time Bud's bruised face. Hardy nudged at him with his foot. "Get up and ready to ride."

Bud groaned.

Hardy squatted to shake Bud's shoulders. "Get up and ride."

"I can't," he said, wriggling his legs and contorting his face.

"Sure you can, Bud." He pulled him to his feet and aimed him toward his pinto.

Bud realized his hands were now tied behind his back. "I can't ride like this." Bud stumbled a moment from the pain as Hardy pushed him toward his horse.

"Sure you can, Bud, because you're going with me."

"What about breakfast?"

"It was good," Hardy answered curtly.

"I didn't get any."

Hardy shoved Bud again and he stumbled toward his pinto. "You're not getting any more food until I break your spirit."

"Bastard."

Hardy ignored his curse and grabbed Bud by the arm and steered him to the pinto. At the side of the horse, Hardy commanded him, "Give me your foot."

Bud stood stubbornly with both feet planted on the ground.

"Hell, Bud, there are a couple ways to do this." Hardy grabbed Bud's leg under the knee and lifted it suddenly.

Bud lost his balance and collapsed backward. He cried out in pain when his head struck the ground. "Okay, okay," he shouted. "Just don't shove me again as sore as I am."

Hardy pulled Bud up, maneuvered him to the saddle, lifted his foot into the stirrup and helped him climb gingerly into the leather. Once Bud was in place, Hardy unhobbled the pinto and led him by the reins to Hardy's horse.

After tying Bud's reins to a cinch on his own saddle and unhobbling his claybank, Hardy climbed into the saddle and angled through the trees back to the Fort Smith road, approaching the road beyond the stream where he had left it last evening. As he neared the road, he heard the noise of a couple of wagons headed toward Boggy Depot. He let them pass and waited until he heard the wagons splash through the stream before he led his captive onto the road.

The morning was still cool and the air prickled his skin. The cool air would help him stay awake, but he must be careful that he didn't let Bud take advantage of his exhaustion.

As he reached the road, he turned the horses toward Fort Smith, then saw something that meant trouble. A man on a black horse. The rider clung to the shadows of the trees on the near side of the stream. Hardy knew this was the same horse that had been trailing them yesterday, even though he had barely gotten a glimpse of it.

Hardy pretended not to see the rider and turned toward Eastman's Mill on the Fort Smith road. Bud was still groggy in the saddle, but likely alert enough to tip off this silent shadow behind him as he had done the day before. Hardy must not let Bud catch on or he would never get the drop on this strange man.

Hardy stared a quarter of a mile down the road, noting the gentle curve that would offer him the chance he needed to get the drop on this shadow. But what to do with Bud? Hardy twisted around in his saddle to check

•

on Bud who seemed oblivious to everything. Hardy's gaze was just long enough to catch a glimpse of the solitary man on their trail.

If Hardy pulled into the woods again, he feared Bud would sound the alarm like yesterday and this quarry would escape again. Hardy didn't have time to gag him. He had but one answer to the problem and it might create the distraction necessary for him to get the jump on the stranger. Hardy figured he had a two-minute lead on the man.

As Hardy approached the curve he slowed up enough for Bud's trailing pinto to draw closer. After glancing back over his shoulder and seeing that the trees screened him from view, Hardy drew back the reins of his mount, jerked his pistol from his holster and slammed the barrel up against the side of Bud's head. Bud's eyes rolled back and he tumbled into the middle of the road, startling both horses for a moment. After Hardy got control of his mount, he led the pinto quickly into the trees, dismounted and tied both mounts. Pulling his pistol, he edged back to the tree line and waited for his unannounced companion to round the curve.

When the rider appeared, he rode along the edge of the trees skirting the opposite side of the road. The black horse lifted then shook its head at the sight of Bud sprawled in the road. When the rider spotted Bud, he glanced down the road, then behind him as well. For a moment he seemed puzzled, though Hardy could not be sure because his features were obscured by the morning shadows. He wore a black long coat and a black hat with a wide brim that further shielded his face.

The rider approached Bud, then pulled back on the reins harder than was necessary to stop the black gelding's progress. Again the rider looked both ways down the road, then slowly dismounted, tying his reins around his left wrist as he moved to Bud and squatted over him. The man rolled Bud over on his back and shook his head.

Hardy stepped from the trees and cocked his gun.

The metallic snap caught the man's attention and he looked up straight into the barrel of Hardy's Colt. "This is the law. Raise your hands and state your business."

Slowly, the man arose, his dark eyes narrow as his lips. He kept his hands wide of waist, but he didn't raise them to his shoulders. He spread his legs wide so that the long coat fell behind the twin holsters riding on his hips.

Hardy watched his right hand as he wriggled his fingers. That would be the hand he made his move with since his reins were tied around his left wrist.

"Raise your hands," Hardy repeated.

The man stared at him, then shook his left hand, the black horse dancing away from him, pulling him slightly. He answered through drawn lips, "I raise them too high, the horse will spook," he said.

"State your name and business," Hardy commanded.

"Temp Whitesides. I was trying to help a man in need." He toed at Bud, who groaned at the boot in his ribs.

"You been following me for two days."

Whitesides shrugged.

"You turned tail and ran yesterday."

"Don't know what you're talking about." Whitesides wriggled his fingers and gauged Hardy.

"You can't beat me." Hardy shook his gun at Whitesides's chest to make his point.

"Beat you, why the hell should I be trying to beat you? I don't even know who the hell you are."

"Deputy U.S. Marshal Doyle Hardy."

Whitesides showed no emotion at Hardy's announcement.

"You must be the one whose own boy's put a five hundred dollar reward on his head. How's it feel knowing there's money on your head for a change?"

Hardy tried to remember any outstanding warrants on Whitesides, but he had let go of all that when he retired, never figuring to be back in The Nations again.

"Five hundred dollars could sure come in handy for a man like me," Whitesides said.

With his free hand, Hardy pointed to Bud. "That's my boy. Does he look like he has five hundred dollars?"

Whitesides shrugged. "Wouldn't matter if he didn't. Being the man who killed Doyle Hardy would be enough reward. It'd make me a tough man."

"No," Hardy answered, "it'd make you a marked man." Hardy waved his gun at Whitesides. "Now, I want you to unbuckle your gun belt and let it drop to the ground."

Very cautiously, Whitesides moved his right hand to the belt buckle and carefully loosened it. He held the gun belt at his side, then suddenly flung it at Hardy, who jumped out of the way and aimed at Whitesides, but fired wide.

At the abrupt move and the gun's explosion, the black gelding tossed its head and danced away, pulling Whitesides off stride for a moment as his right hand disappeared into the pocket of his black riding coat.

Hardy saw the right pocket suddenly stiffen.

The whole side of Whitesides's riding coat lifted.

Hardy grimaced.

Whitesides had a pistol in his pocket!

Hardy dove to the ground and rolled.

Whitesides's coat seemed to explode in a puff of smoke.

As he hit the ground on his left shoulder, Hardy grimaced at the pain.

Whitesides cursed at the miss and jerked at his pistol and his coat pocket.

Hardy rolled onto his stomach and lifted his pistol at his assailant. He drew a bead on Whitesides's stomach.

Whitesides screamed curses as the gun snagged in the lining of his pocket and the panicked black gelding jerked at his arm. With a rip of cloth, he managed to pull the gun free. He squeezed off another shot, but the jittery horse fouled his aim.

Hardy pulled on the trigger and his Colt exploded in a cloud of smoke.

Whitesides screamed at the splotch of red that suddenly appeared on his belly. He fired his own gun wildly at the air, the black gelding killing his aim and almost jerking his arm from his shoulder.

Hardy fired again.

Whitesides staggered, then fell to the ground. "Damn you," he scowled, his lips bubbling blood, the gun dropping from his hand.

"You'll collect no reward," Hardy said, standing up and dusting himself off.

As he neared Eastman's Mill, Hardy saw the reminders of the bad trip to Boggy Depot. He passed the carcass of his gray; its saddle had been taken along with the saddlebags, bedroll, bridle and carbine. Hardy shook his head. What had been a damn fine horse was nothing but carrion now. Nearby were the remains of the two LeHew horses Hardy had shot.

When he passed the tree marked with a blazed *B* denoting the Boykin place, Hardy glanced over his shoulder at Bud, who showed no sign of remorse at how he had treated the Boykin girl. Hardy wondered if the girl had recovered from how Bud had treated her. She should have, but Bud had a way of sweet-talking women and making them take leave of their senses. Boone Dillon had been rumored to have such a way with words around women. Hardy was glad to pass the Boykin place without seeing any of the family.

As he rode across the plank bridge that led to Eastman's Mill, Hardy lifted the gun belt that had belonged to Temp Whitesides. At first he was tempted to throw the whole outfit into the river, but he carried little spare ammunition since the LeHew brothers had killed his gray. Hardy hooked the gun belt back over his saddle horn and pulled each .45 from its holster, tossing each over the bridge. The guns landed with a thunk and then disappeared beneath the water. No sense in having extra guns around, guns that Bud could use.

Behind him Bud periodically groaned from the pain and from the discomfort of riding with his hands tied behind his back. It had been a rough day on Bud but a rougher one on Temp Whitesides. His body was strapped down to the black gelding, its reins tied to the pinto's saddle. Travel had been slow and Hardy didn't see any prospect of the pace improving as long as he had to drag Bud and a dead man along.

As he crossed the bridge into Eastman's Mill, word of his return and his cargo seemed to spread. Quickly, the handful of folks who called Eastman's Mill home were out on the street, pointing and gossiping.

Hardy pulled up in the middle of the road and recognized Pernell Eastman stepping away from the mill itself. The mill operator waved his hand with the three missing fingertips. "You made it back," he said to Doyle Hardy as he studied Bud. "Old man Boykin'll breathe a little easier now. He kept fearing your boy would return to steal his girl away in the night."

Hardy shook his head. "He's going to jail."

Eastman jerked his thumb toward the body. "Who's that?"

"A man who called himself Temp Whitesides. He tried to collect my son's five hundred dollar reward."

"Bastard," Bud grumbled at his father.

Hardy ignored the profanity and asked a favor of Eastman. "Think you can build a pine box for Temp Whitesides and see that he's buried?"

"If you're paying."

Hardy shook his head. "No money for that. I don't get any money when I bring them in dead. But I tell you what. The black gelding and Whitesides's gear ought to cover the cost and more."

Eastman studied the gelding. "I can arrange something."

"Then he's all yours." Hardy wondered how many of Marshal Jacob Yoes's rules he had just violated.

Eastman stepped around Bud's pinto and untied the black's reins from Bud's saddle, slowly leading the gelding to Hardy. "The LeHews have been searching the road between here and Skullyville, looking for you. They're plenty mad about you killing their horses. I'd be careful if I were you."

"Always am," Hardy replied. He started to move on, but looked at the sky and saw it was near lunchtime. He might just as well eat at Eastman's Mill, rather than try to eat something on the trail. "Any place to eat a decent meal?"

A man, attired in a stained undershirt and ripped jeans, stepped up to Hardy's horse. "I cook in the building with no sign and you're welcome to eat, if you like."

"How long until we can eat?"

"Give me a few minutes. Is it a deal?"

Hardy nodded.

The cook scampered toward the unmarked building.

Hardy nudged his horse forward, leaving Pernell Eastman to attend to the body.

Bud seemed suddenly invigorated by the thought of food. "We will have food for lunch?"

Hardy nodded.

"How am I gonna eat, my hands being tied behind me."

"Like a dog, Bud, like a dog. If that don't satisfy you, then I might take it upon myself to feed you like I used to do when you were a baby."

Hardy tied the horses and helped Bud down and inside the eatery. It was small, but cleaner on the inside than it was on the outside. The cook forked over boiled beef, fresh bread and some red beans. When Hardy was done eating, he fed Bud, who complained so much that Hardy threatened to take him away without another bite. The whining stopped.

Hardy was tired from the half day's ride and from Bud's attempt to strangle him last night. The burn around his neck still ached and didn't show any promise of letting up.

While the food seemed to invigorate Bud, it seemed to make Hardy drowsy. He would have to be on his guard once they left. The closer they came to Fort Smith, the more desperate Bud would become. He would see his freedom draining away. And then somewhere out there rode the LeHew brothers, just biding their time for a chance at revenge. Now Hardy remembered the strain of riding The Nations. He was getting too old for this type of work, nursemaiding prisoners.

Bud ate every bite Hardy fed him voraciously. "Better than your damn sausage and biscuits."

"You better eat plenty 'cause you won't be getting any supper."

His mouth full, Bud laughed. "And you won't be getting any sleep tonight. I'll get all the sleep I need and if I wake up and you're still awake, I'll get more sleep. But if you're asleep, I'll get you."

"I trusted you last night, left you where you could get rest. That won't happen tonight. You'll be the one that'll have trouble getting to sleep." Hardy shoved a spoon of beans in Bud's mouth, gagging him.

Bud coughed and spat beans down the front of his shirt.

"You should take better care of your fancy clothes."

"Bastard," Bud growled.

"You've had enough to eat." Hardy threw the spoon down in the tin plate. He quickly paid the cook and dispensed with the receipt. He was ready to get away from Eastman's Mill. He jerked Bud up from his bench seat and shoved him toward the eatery door. Bud smashed into it, turning around and cursing.

Hardy answered with a sarcastic grin. "I get a little irritable when I don't get a good night's sleep." Hardy shoved him aside and lifted the catch on the door.

Bud cursed him again as Hardy pushed him outside. He stumbled and almost fell in front of his pinto.

Hardy stepped to him. "It'd been a lot easier on us both, Bud, if I'd just whipped you when you needed it years ago. Maybe I'd kept you from setting a date with the hangman."

With his fancy stitched boots, Bud kicked dirt at Hardy. "You ain't got me to Fort Smith yet."

"Nope, but I've gotten men a lot meaner and a lot smarter than you to Fort Smith." Hardy walked to Bud to help him into the saddle, but Bud resisted his effort to lift his boot into the stirrup. "Dammit, Bud, I'm running out of patience and places to hit you to make you understand. Are you going to cooperate or not?"

"If you'd tie my hands in front of me instead of behind me, I could manage myself."

"You should've thought about that last night when you tried to strangle me."

Bud lifted his knee and Hardy guided his boot into the stirrup, then boosted him into the saddle. He untied the pinto's reins from the hitching rail and retied them to his own saddle, then released his gelding and mounted.

Most of the residents of Eastman's Mill stopped their activities and watched Hardy lead his son away. As Hardy surveyed the spectators, he saw a couple of sawdust-covered mill men straighten up from a pine box they were nailing together for the late Temp Whitesides.

Travel was slowed by Bud's uneasy balance on the pinto and by Hardy's periodic retreats into woods to watch for anyone who might be trailing. When the sun began to wane to the west, Hardy pulled off the trail and led Bud's pinto into the woods. He was looking for a special site to camp, a site with a strong oak tree.

A half mile from the road he found what he was looking for, an oak tree atop a flat-topped rise that gave him as good a view of the surrounding land as was possible in wooded terrain.

"Here's where we'll camp," Hardy announced, as he stopped his horse beneath the oak tree and dismounted. He helped Bud down from the saddle, then cross-hobbled the pinto. "You might want to walk around, stretch you legs a little."

Bud laughed. "I'll have plenty of time to stretch out when I hit my bedroll."

"I wouldn't be so sure of that, Bud."

Cursing, Bud walked away, then turned and watched Hardy as he began to hobble and unsaddle his own horse. "You'd make a damn fine stable hand as good as you unsaddle horses."

Hardy dropped his saddle on the ground, then went to Bud's pinto and removed the bedroll which he tossed beside his saddle.

"That's my bedroll," Bud complained.

"Not tonight," Hardy replied, settling down on Bud's blanket and leaning against his saddle as he opened the bundle of sausage and biscuits. He grabbed a patty of meat and a hard biscuit, neither of which had improved with age. He began to chew.

"Where's my supper?" Bud demanded.

"I told you back at Eastman's Mill you weren't getting any."

"Bastard. When are you going to unsaddle my pinto?"

"I'm not."

Bud twisted around and shook his bound hands at Hardy. "I damn sure can't with my hands like this."

"I told you you might ought to stretch your legs."

"Bastard," he said.

When Hardy finished his meager supper, he leaned over and uncinched from his saddle the rope Noah Barnes had bought for him. The rope was stiff but the small diameter made it supple enough for Hardy's needs. He took the end, made a loop, then began to wrap tight coils of rope around the top of the loop. Out of the corner of his eye, he watched Bud's face pale as he realized Hardy was constructing a hangman's noose.

Finishing the noose, Hardy tossed it at his son's feet so Bud would not miss it and its sinister threat.

"What's that for?" Bud demanded.

"I intend to get some sleep tonight, Bud."

Bud thrust out his chest, determined to continue his defiance, but his swagger was dimmed by the uncertainty of Hardy's plan for the noose.

"Want to go for a ride, Bud? A short ride?"

Bud shook his head as Hardy pushed himself up from his blanket. "You're not gonna hang me?" His voice rang with panic.

"No, Bud, not at all." Hardy moved to the pinto. "Now come over here and mount up, with my help of course."

His eyes widening, Bud took a tentative step and stopped cold. "What are you trying to do?"

"Get a good night's sleep, Bud, where you won't bother me."

"What's the noose for?" There was desperation in his voice.

"You coming or not?"

Bud stood as stiffly as if his boots had taken root to the earth.

Hardy shook his head. "Too bad, Bud, too bad." He picked up the rope end with the sinister noose. He stepped toward Bud.

Bud uprooted his boots from the soil and backed away. "What are you doing?"

Bud spun around to run, but Hardy tossed the noose at his feet, tripping him up. Bud fell flat on his face. When he rolled over, his nose spurted blood and his eyes seemed as wide as saucers, especially when Hardy slipped the noose over his head and tightened the stiff and prickly hemp against his neck. Bud screamed, more from fear than from pain.

"What are you doing?" The defiance in Bud's voice was replaced by desperation.

"Get a good night's sleep. Now get up." Hardy tugged on the noose and Bud slowly got to his feet. When he stood, Hardy saw his knees were quivering.

"What are you doing? Tell me," Bud begged.

"You scared, Bud? You ever thought this might be

how Molina felt when you attacked her? Someone she thought loved her was going to kill her. Did she scream, Bud? And poor Daniel, did he know what was going on? Did he start crying and screaming, too, because you were hurting his mama?"

Bud's eyes watered over, then he began to sob. "I was drunk. I didn't know. Please don't kill me!"

Hardy led him to his pinto. "Now, I'll help you mount up."

"No, please don't do this. I deserve a trial, a judge with a jury."

"Did Molina get a judge and jury, Bud? What about Daniel? He was an innocent little fellow, never did anything to anybody. You took away so much of his life."

"Please don't," Bud begged.

Hardy slapped him across the face with the back of his hand. "Don't cry like Daniel did. Be a man."

Bud's knees turned to mush and he staggered against the pinto's saddle. Hardy propped him up, forcing his hand-stitched boot into the stirrup and then pushing him up into the saddle. Still holding the rope, Hardy took the pinto's reins and led the animal beneath a sturdy branch of the oak. The hobbled gelding inched ahead until Hardy stopped him beneath the branch near the tree trunk.

"Please don't hang me." The starch was all gone from his voice.

Hardy tossed the rope over the branch and let it fall over the opposite side in front of Bud.

Bud's shoulders slumped further until he leaned forward. He began to gag and retch, but nothing remained in his stomach for him to lose, except his nerves.

With the twilight thickening, Hardy grabbed the

end of the rope from the ground and looped it around the tree trunk, then pulled it snug.

Bud was jerked from his slump by the tightening rope. Against his will, he straightened in the saddle. "No, no," he whispered.

Hardy loosened the rope to give Bud about six inches of slack, then tied it around the tree trunk.

"This ain't right," Bud said quietly for fear of spooking his horse.

"Neither was killing Molina and Daniel or trying to strangle me last night. Now, your horse is hobbled and won't go far unless he's spooked. So if you want to yell and try to keep me awake, go ahead."

"This ain't right," Bud sobbed.

"A lot of things aren't right in The Nations, Bud. This is just one of them."

"What if I fall asleep?"

"It'll be a long sleep, Bud." Hardy turned for his bedroll. "Good night, Bud."

20

Come morning, Hardy awoke early. Bud was still atop the horse, though the pinto had inched forward a bit and Bud was sitting on the animal's rump, his boots wedged in the stirrups which were pulled back against the flank of the animal by Bud's desperate efforts to stay aboard the horse.

Hardy arose and stretched, then strolled over to the pinto, grabbing it by the bridle and easing it back until Bud could slide back in the saddle.

Bud slumped forward, saying nothing, merely shaking his head.

Next Hardy moved around behind the horse to the tree trunk and untied the rope. Returning to Bud's side, he grabbed the noose end of the rope and jerked the remainder over the tree limb.

Bud sighed.

Hardy could not tell if he was a broken man or merely an exhausted one.

"Bastard," Bud whispered.

Merely exhausted, Hardy realized. "Lean over," he ordered.

Bud lowered his head far enough for Hardy to remove the noose.

Hardy drew the rope into a coil as he returned to the bedroll. After rolling up the bedding, he took a sausage and biscuit for himself and another set for Bud from the food bundle.

"Are you ever going to get me down?" Bud said, his eyes heavy with exhaustion.

"What?" Hardy said.

When Bud opened his mouth to repeat his question, Hardy stuffed it with the biscuit and sausage. Though angered, Bud savored the taste of the food and did not spit it out.

Hardy took the reins of Bud's hobbled pinto and led it to his gelding. Hardy saddled and loaded the claybank with Bud's carbine and bedroll.

As soon as Bud swallowed his breakfast, he shouted at Hardy. "Ain't you gonna let me get some shut-eye?"

"Sure," Hardy said, "as much as you want in the saddle. We've one more night on the trail and after that you can sleep as long as the warden will allow."

"Bastard."

Hardy tied the pinto's reins to his saddle, then unhobbled both horses and mounted.

"What about something to drink?" Bud demanded.

"When we come to a clear-water stream."

"No wonder you're so hated in The Nations."

Hardy shrugged. "Law-abiding folks don't hate me. They may not like me but they don't hate me, not after as many bad men as I've cleared out for them." He angled the horses through the trees for the Fort Smith road.

Bud mumbled as they rode. But by the time they

reached the road, Bud was quiet except for his heavy breathing and occasional snores. By midmorning, Hardy met a regular traffic of men on horseback and in wagons, a few loaded with families. All the travelers stared as if Hardy was leading a circus parade. Men riding in pairs looked from the badge on Hardy's chest to Bud, riding stiffly on his pinto, and whispered to themselves that this was Doyle Hardy, the U.S. Deputy Marshal who had sought and captured his own son. Wide-eyed kids clumped together in wagons giggled and pointed at Bud as they passed.

Hardy looked over his shoulder at Bud, who looked like a riding corpse. His head was still swollen from the day before when Hardy had slammed him with his revolver. His eye was bruised and swollen. His face was caked with blood from landing on his nose when he tried to run from the noose last night. And his clothes were splotched with blood, dirt and sweat.

They traveled slowly enough that several riders passed them. Hardy knew it was dangerous not to pick up the pace because word of their approach could tip off the LeHew brothers or other possible assassins up ahead. Even so, Bud's body was battered and at times, thought Hardy, his spirit was broken. Hardy had been through enough with Bud without having to push him harder on what was his final trip—except for the walk to the gallows and the step into eternity.

For all his concerns about Bud—and he could no longer tell if they were real or a father's guilt—Hardy knew of another reason the pace was slow. He wanted to stop by Emma Sims's place and have a few minutes with her. For all the tribulations of this journey, his time with her had been worthwhile. He had forgotten how a woman could make a man feel needed, not just physically, but emotionally as well. That bond between man and woman was as much a part of God's plan as the sky overhead and the trees by his side. For all the time he had spent over the years dealing with the godless, Hardy had come to respect the godly.

Hardy stopped at the first creek crossing so the horses and his prisoner could drink. "I'll wash your face, Bud. You're frightening the kids that pass."

"Why the hell should I care?" Bud shot back.

"Because you want to get a good night's sleep, don't you?" Hardy patted the noose cinched to his saddle horn as he climbed out of the saddle, then helped Bud down.

Hardy splashed water on Bud's face and scrubbed at the dried blood which dissolved into a pink liquid that drained back into the creek, then disappeared in the moving water.

Hardy helped Bud back in the saddle, then took a drink for himself. The water was sweet, cool and refreshing. He wondered if it were the water or his approach to Emma Sims's place that suddenly invigorated him. At the present speed, he figured to reach her farm a couple of hours before dark, maybe in time for supper. Remounting, Hardy resumed his sad journey.

After noon, Hardy ate another sausage and biscuit, then stuffed the last of each into Bud's mouth. Bud chewed slowly to get every last morsel of flavor before swallowing. Now they were without food. If Emma didn't have something for them to eat, it would be a long night. Hardy didn't plan to stay at her place. He wanted desperately to see her, but feared an overnight stay might bring her trouble.

By late afternoon he had passed Signal Hill and

was nearing the crossing of the creek where the two moonshiners had hidden their still. He wondered if his threat had kept them miles away from Emma's place or if they had resumed their distilling nearby.

The sun was drooping in the western sky as Hardy approached the Sims place. He sat up in his saddle, straightened his hat and nudged his gelding into a soft trot. The gelding's pace jerked the pinto into a faster gait and drew curses from Bud.

"What the hell are you doing, trying to knock me out of the saddle?"

"Like you dumped the Boykin girl?" Hardy shot back. "Mind your manners, Bud Hardy, or you'll go without supper or sleep again."

Bud grunted.

Hardy turned off the road and approached the farmhouse and barn. Out in the corral, Hardy spotted the little ones feeding the livestock. At the sound of Hardy's approach, the two boys jumped for the wooden rail fence and climbed it for a better view. They paused a few seconds until they recognized the rider, then bounced off the fence and bounded for the house, screaming, "Big Ma, Big Ma!"

No sooner did they barge in the front door, than Emma Sims rushed out, wiping her hands on her apron and waving with joy. It did Hardy's heart good to see her excitement. Then her smile became subdued and her gesture not nearly as exuberant. Hardy pulled back on the reins and took off his hat as his horse came to a stop in front of her porch.

"Good to see you, Emma Sims. And the little ones, too."

The two boys giggled.

As Hardy dismounted, Emma darted off the porch and ran for him, throwing her arms around his shoulders. "I had heard you might have been shot. I was worried with fright."

She placed her cheek against his chest and nuzzled at him for a moment, then broke away. "This is not right," she whispered, "in front of your son. He is your son?"

Hardy nodded.

"I'm sorry." She shook Hardy's hand. "Will you stay the night?"

Hardy shook his head. "The LeHews may be riding these parts."

The bigger of the boys stepped off the porch. "They passed by here early afternoon. Different horses, but the same men."

"We'll tie our horses around back, out of sight and try not to bring you any trouble," Hardy said.

"You do not bring trouble, you bring the law."

Hardy led his horse around to the back and tied it to a hitching ring, then untied Bud's pinto and retied it to the ring as well. Hardy helped Bud off his pinto.

"We can't stay, Emma, but we could use a bit of supper. We've eaten mostly sausage and biscuits since we left Boggy Depot."

"I can fix you supper," Emma Sims answered as she studied Bud. "He is bruised and hurt, does he need attention?" As she glanced at Hardy, her hand flew to her mouth and her eyes widened. She moved quickly to Hardy. "You are hurt!" She lifted her hand and touched the scabbed crease where Bud had tried to strangle him. "What happened?"

"Nothing," Hardy said, not wishing to admit that Bud had gotten the drop on him or that his son would do such a thing.

Emma Sims turned back to Bud. "Shame on you for bringing dishonor upon your father's good name. He is a decent man."

"Shut up, squaw," Bud blurted out.

Instantly, Hardy drew back his hand and slapped Bud across his sore cheek.

Bud yelped. "Bastard!"

Hardy slapped him again. "If you want anything to eat, you best shut your mouth and behave."

Bud's eyes narrowed in anger, but he said nothing else.

"Apologize," Hardy demanded.

"It is okay," Emma Sims said, grabbing Hardy's arm.

"Apologize," Hardy insisted.

Bud merely shook his head.

"Please," Emma pleaded, "it is okay. He is not the man that his father is."

Hardy gritted his teeth at her words. Maybe Bud was the man that his father was, maybe Bud was Boone Dillon's offspring. How could a man so vile be his own son?

"Please," Emma repeated. "I must make you supper so you can be on your way, if that is what you want."

"It is."

In spite of Bud's insults, Emma stepped to him, took his arm and turned him around where she could see the leather bindings on his wrists. The leather dug into his flesh, raw in places. "Must he be tied so tightly?"

Hardy slowly nodded his head. "I lost all my wrist shackles."

"It's a shame to keep a boy bound like this."

"For all his sorry looks, he's a mean one, Emma."

"I'm sorry for you, Doyle Hardy, that you must carry the burden of your son's wrongdoing." She retreated into the kitchen.

Putting his hat back on, Hardy turned to Bud. "You best walk around and stretch while you still have the chance. You won't get much sleep tonight."

Bud cocked his head and stood there staring, mocking Hardy with his gaze.

"Suit yourself." Hardy went to his saddle and untied the gun belt he had taken from Temp Whitesides. He began to pull the bullets from the cartridge loops and put them in his pocket. He counted out thirty-seven bullets in addition to those he had remaining in his own belt. He wished he hadn't lost his mount and extra ammunition against the LeHew brothers. When he was done with the extra gun belt, he tossed it to the little ones who had stood watching him the entire time. They laughed, especially when they wrapped the gun belt around the two of them and buckled it.

Shortly the aroma of frying salt pork seeped out of the kitchen. Hardy felt his stomach knot in anticipation of supper. He glanced at Bud edging toward his horse and carbine. "Get away from the horses, Bud. And the carbine."

Shaking his head, Bud moved back. "Bastard," he said under his breath and the little ones giggled.

Hardy went about checking his and Bud's mounts, inspecting their legs and their shoes, nodding satisfaction that everything looked like it would make it to Fort Smith. With each passing moment, the aromas from the kitchen grew more enticing until Hardy thought he could barely wait for supper.

"Come in, little ones," called Emma from the kitchen and the two boys proudly entered, the gift gun belt buckled around them both. She pretended to scold them and they laughed until she put them to setting the table. "Won't be long," Emma called.

Hardy edged over to Bud and whispered to him. "You best behave in there or I'll teach you more of the manners I should've taught you years ago. You'll eat last, Bud, because I've got no leverage on your manners once you've eaten."

Bud shrugged. "It ain't my job to care what the hell you do. You still haven't gotten me to Fort Smith."

"Yes, sir, Bud Hardy, you're right, but you're a hell of a lot closer to Judge Parker's court than you were two days ago."

"Supper's ready," Emma called from her kitchen.

"Remember your manners," Hardy instructed, then grabbed Bud by the elbow, twisted him around and marched him to the back door.

The boys were already seated as Emma pulled a large pan of biscuits from the stove.

Hardy helped Bud into a chair, then seated himself to Bud's right so he could not make a grab for the pistol on the marshal's right hip. He took off his hat and put it in the empty chair to his right.

Never had Hardy seen set before him a platter with so much salt pork. In addition to that, Emma had a huge bowl of skillet-fried potatoes, a vast bowl of gravy, some creamed corn and a dish of butter.

Emma nodded for Hardy to help himself. As hungry as he was, he didn't need a second invitation. He piled strips of bacon, four biscuits, mounds of potatoes and generous helpings of corn on his plate, then covered the bacon and biscuits with ladles of gravy.

As he dug into his supper, Emma nodded for the little ones and they began to fill their plates. "What about your son?" Emma asked.

"He can wait until I'm done because I will have to feed him."

Emma stood up from her chair and walked around the table. "I can do that." She loaded his plate with food and picked up his fork, stabbing a round of potato and a fragment of bacon. She smiled at him, but Bud stared beyond Emma toward her shotgun propped in the corner by the door.

Hardy noted Bud's fixation on the shotgun but was less worried about that than the manners he showed Emma Sims. Bud ate voraciously, but never offered her thanks or even acknowledgment. Patient Emma seemed not the least bit affected by Bud's sullen demeanor. She only wanted to help.

When Hardy could hold no more, Bud kept eating, consuming food like a locomotive firebox takes on wood. Finally, Bud nodded his satisfaction.

"I did not have time to fix any sweets, but I have biscuits and butter with jelly," Emma said.

Hardy looked outside at the evening twilight setting in.

"We should be putting a little distance between you and us."

Emma seemed disappointed, averting her eyes from his. "I'm glad that you stopped. I enjoyed preparing your meal."

Hardy arose from his chair, grabbed his hat and helped Bud up.

"Come see me again. You are always welcome."

Hardy smiled. He wanted so to take her in his arms for a moment and hug her, but he was still a married man. He turned Bud toward the door and marched him outside, helping him into the saddle, then untying the pinto's reins and hooking them to his own saddle.

Quickly, Hardy mounted, but Emma ran to him, taking his hand in hers and kissing it gently.

"So long, Emma."

He turned and led Bud away.

"Look's like someone else has been getting a little on the side." Bud laughed.

"For that, Bud, you won't get much sleep tonight."

21

They made about three miles in the gathering
darkness before turning off the Fort Smith
road and into the woods. Hardy had a nagging
suspicion that he was being followed. Sure enough, not
more than a couple minutes after he had slipped into
the trees with Bud, a solitary rider slowly approached
along the narrow road. Hardy rested his hand on the
butt of his revolver. In the sparse light, Hardy saw a
vague shadow pass, but the rider rode on without slowing and Hardy dismissed him as a casual traveler.

Hardy led Bud further into the woods. Not fifty
yards from the road he found a tree about the right
height. Hardy dismounted and hobbled both horses,
then untied the rope from his saddle.

"You ain't gonna hang me again?" Bud shouted.

"Shut up, Bud. I told you to mind your manners
back there."

"Why, you sweet on the squaw?"

Hardy grabbed Bud's arm and pulled him over
until he could get the noose around his neck. Hardy
shoved him back upright in the saddle.

"Damn you to hell," Bud screamed as Hardy led his hobbled pinto beneath the tree.

Hardy tossed the rope over a sturdy branch and snugged it tight around his son's neck, strangling the next insult on Bud's lips. Hardy moved to the tree trunk and tied the rope to the bottom. "Remember not to spook your horse or you'll have a long sleep."

"Bastard," Bud scowled through clenched lips.

"I should've straightened you out a long time ago, Bud. It's easier to set a boy on the right path, even after he's strayed, than it is to set a man straight."

Hardy walked back to his gelding and fumbled in the dark to unfasten Bud's bedroll. He tossed the bedroll on the best spot of level ground he could find and began to unfurl his bedding. Behind him he could hear Bud still mumbling profanity at him. Hardy cut loose a shrill whistle, which startled the two horses, both taking small hobbled steps.

Bud gasped. "Don't do that or my pinto will bolt."

"Then shut your damned mouth, Bud."

"Okay, okay, just scoot the pinto back under me so I'm full in the saddle."

Hardy moved from his bedroll to the pinto and eased the nervous animal back a step or two. "That better?"

Bud nodded.

As Hardy moved back to his bedroll, he heard the sound of voices drifting clearly through the night air. He suddenly worried how clearly his conversation and shrill whistle had carried to the road. He cursed that he was responsible for giving away his hiding spot. That wouldn't matter unless the men were looking for him.

Then he heard a sound that sent a chill up his back. It was a voice he recognized.

"That whistle came from nearby," said Satch LeHew.

"They left the road near here," said another.

"Yeah," Satch gloated, "I told you we needed to keep an eye on that squaw's farm. Wasn't I right?"

"So what," mumbled his other brother, "once we get Doyle Hardy we can go back and have a little fun with the widder squaw."

All three men laughed sinisterly.

Hardy eased away from his bedroll toward his gelding, pulling Bud's carbine from its scabbard, then leading his horse beyond Bud and his pinto.

As Hardy eased by Bud's pinto, Bud suddenly screamed out a warning. "Satch, he's up here."

The frightened pinto lunged ahead on hobbled legs, running into Hardy who grabbed his bridle and steadied the horse, then backed him under Bud.

"Is that you, Bud?" called Satch LeHew. "We're coming up."

Hardy heard the horses turn off the road and start into the woods. He abandoned the pinto and eased to a tree for cover.

"Don't leave me," Bud whispered in a panic to Hardy.

"Where are you, Bud?" called Satch LeHew.

"He's got a gun," Bud called out as loudly as he thought he could without spooking his pinto. "And he's got a noose around my neck. If you stampede the horse, it'll hang me."

"That's a damn shame, Bud, that your horse would run off from you like you ran off from us when we ambushed your pa."

Hardy twisted around. "Shut up, Bud, or you'll kill yourself." Hardy looked back at the road, focusing hard on the darkness, trying to pick out the approaching men. He could hear the footsteps of their horses and their whispered instructions.

"Don't let him circle us like he did last time," Satch said, "and keep up with our own horses."

Bud spoke nervously. "You're getting closer."

"Shut up," Hardy growled at Bud.

Hardy saw a tongue of flame and heard the explosion of a gun. He took aim at the location, but was distracted by Bud's scream behind him.

"No," Bud cried, "you're scaring my—" His words died with the excited stamp of his pinto and the creak of the limb overhead.

Hardy heard a gurgle and realized the pinto had walked out from under Bud. Hardy threw down his carbine and darted to the tree, just as a couple more shots rang out and echoed through the woods.

"Bud, Bud," he cried. Hardy raced past the writhing figure and aimed for the tree trunk. He grabbed the rope and fumbled for the knot. It would not give. More shots came from behind him, whizzing overhead. His fingernails dug into the stiff rope without success. "Dammit," he screamed. "I'm trying, Bud, I'm trying."

The knot would not give.

Another shot exploded and Hardy caught a glimpse of the flash of light. The LeHews were drawing nearer.

The rope clung tight and Bud seemed to have given up the fight.

His knife! That was Hardy's only chance to save Bud.

Hardy shoved his hand into his britches pocket, jerking out the knife and scattering at his feet many of the bullets he had saved from Temp Whitesides's gun belt. Hardy fumbled to open the sharp blade, finally pulling it free and slicing at the rope against the tree trunk. For a moment it seemed as if he were trying to saw through a railroad tie, but finally the blade succeeded and the rope jerked loose, Bud collapsing in a heap on the ground behind him.

He scrambled to Bud, as shots from the LeHews punctuated the darkness. Hardy hurriedly loosened the noose from Bud's neck. Bud gasped for air and flailed his arms.

Grabbing Bud under the shoulders, Hardy pulled him behind the tree for cover, the rope trailing them like a long snake in the dark.

With Bud shielded behind the tree, Hardy pulled his revolver. He figured he had less than fifty bullets total, too few for a long standoff.

Bud gasped beside him, clawing at the rope and trying to get the full measure of the air he had been denied for several seconds.

Thinking he saw some movement, Hardy squeezed the trigger. His aim drew a scream and a curse.

"That son of a bitch was close," cried one of the LeHews. Several gunshots answered Hardy's.

Hardy decided to bluff. "You boys better throw down your guns and surrender. Things'll go lighter on you if you give up now, than if I have to take you before Judge Parker or kill you."

The LeHews answered with a mocking laugh. "We got you now, you son of a bitch," called Satch LeHew.

"We surrendered to you once and got seven years in prison," yelled another.

"The prison years must not have taken with you."

"Son of a bitch," yelled Satch, followed by a flurry

of shots. "We got all night to wait for you, seeing as how we waited for seven years just for this chance."

"You boys should've turned out right."

"Yeah," Satch LeHew retorted, "like your boy, killing his own woman and son. We ain't killed no babies."

Hardy emptied his revolver at the darkness, realizing it was foolishness and he should conserve his ammunition, but firing anyway at the insult. Quickly, he reloaded the cylinder. He must not fire any more shots as foolishly as the last. He must save his bullets and not let his emotion run wild at their insults. With ammunition depleting, he could not outshoot them. He had to outsmart them.

Bud began to move on the ground beside him, trying to get to his feet. Hardy shoved him back down.

"Stay low or they'll kill you."

Bud shoved Hardy's hand away. "They're after you, not me." His voice was as raspy as the bite of a dull saw.

Hardy sneered. "In the dark they can't tell and they aren't your friends, not after you abandoned them before."

"Least they didn't try to hang me."

"You brought that on yourself, this whole mess." Hardy placed his hand over Bud's mouth to keep him quiet so he could hear the LeHews. Only silence greeted him. The LeHews had likely dismounted.

As he stared into the darkness, Bud bit his hand. "Damn," Hardy cried as he jerked his hand free, then slapped Bud.

"Bastard," Bud shot back with his raspy voice.

Hardy was tempted to knock Bud out, but knew he would have to keep him conscious so they could maneuver around the LeHews. He needed to gag

Bud, but didn't have a kerchief on him. Unless he gagged him, Bud would keep pestering him or revealing whatever position he took.

Bud started kicking at the ground with his boots, trying to help the LeHews find Hardy in the dark.

"You're a fool, Bud, they'll kill you as quick as they will me."

Bud kicked more. "I didn't put them in jail."

"They don't value anybody's life." Hardy paused, then shook his head. "But then neither do you."

Still Bud kicked at the ground.

Ignoring the LeHews for a moment, Hardy straddled Bud's legs and pulled off one boot, then the other.

"What the hell?" Bud rasped.

Hardy flung one of the boots away as a distraction. Two shots were fired at the noise.

Then Hardy had an idea for a gag. He pulled off both of Bud's socks, then knotted them together at the toe. Twisting around, he shoved the knot into Bud's mouth, then tied the ends of the socks behind his neck.

Bud bucked, then gagged at the sour taste in his mouth. He tried to scream, but the sock muffled his effort.

Hardy took Bud's other boot and flung it toward the Fort Smith road. The boot set off another volley of shots.

Behind him Hardy could hear his and Bud's horses slipping deeper into the woods on their hobbled feet. Low on ammunition, Hardy debated whether to make his move in the darkness or wait until light. He knew he couldn't hold out for dawn if he stayed in one place, so he must keep moving. He needed the horses, then came upon an idea of how to use them.

He grabbed the rope around Bud's neck and tugged it. Bud answered with a muffled curse.

"Get up and do what I say," Hardy ordered.

Bud resisted for a moment until Hardy slapped him.

"Stay low. We've got to make it to the horses."

Hardy fired a shot as a distraction, then dragged his reluctant son deeper into the woods after the hobbled horses.

Behind them, the LeHews peppered the woods with lead and curses.

Hardy knew that if he had circled them once to escape, he could circle them again. But this time, the rope around Bud's neck would provide him one more trick.

As he led Bud like a whipped dog through the woods, Hardy gathered in the extra rope in a coil as he neared his gelding.

Behind him he could hear the LeHews, but they seemed confused. "Did we get him?" yelled Satch LeHew.

"Don't know," called another. "I thought I heard someone moving through the trees."

"Bud Hardy," shouted Satch, his voice echoing through the woods, "did we get your old man?"

Bud tried to answer but the gag prevented him.

Hardy grabbed the gelding's reins in the same hand he held the coil of rope and started toward the noise that he knew was the hobbled pinto.

"Think he's trying to circle us again, Satch?" yelled one of his brothers.

"Could be, Clyde," Satch yelled, "but as long as we keep our horses with us, it won't matter."

Reaching the pinto, Hardy slid his pistol in his holster, then pushed Bud in front of him. He draped the coil of rope over the saddle horn on the pinto's saddle. As Hardy moved back toward the road, trying to circle the LeHew brothers, he would use the two horses as shields for himself and Bud.

Hardy wanted the LeHews close enough to fall into the trap he planned, but the trap would require a little time to set up. He just hoped he didn't cut things too finely.

"I hear them," yelled Satch LeHew. "They're still ahead of us."

"Dammit," answered another of his brothers, "I can't see a thing, don't want to shoot each other."

Hardy bent and took the hobbles off both horses and draped them over his shoulders. Standing up, he pushed Bud forward and angled back toward Emma Sims's place, hoping to swing wide enough to get around them.

From Bud's tender step, Hardy knew this walk was rough on his bare feet but Bud had brought this on himself like he had so many of his problems.

"He must be trying to get around us," cried Satch LeHew, "swing wide and fire your guns so we know where we all are."

Hardy glanced back toward the road and saw three successive flashes of light. Dammit. They had already spread out and looked like they would prevent a sweep around their end. But Hardy saw a wide gap between two of the gun flashes. Just maybe he could slip between them as they advanced deeper into the woods.

Gently, Hardy moved the reins and aimed the horses and Bud for the gap between the assailants. Bud stumbled along, seeming to want to make as much noise as he could. Hardy grabbed him by the scruff of the neck and shook him. "You best walk a little quieter."

Hardy pointed the horses for the gap, aiming as near center as he could make out in the darkness. When he was situated where he wanted, he stopped and held his breath. He could hear a man and horse approaching cautiously to his right side and another to his left, both twenty to thirty yards away, as best he could figure. If the horses didn't stamp or whinny and if Bud didn't make any noise, they might stand a chance of sliding behind the LeHew brothers and making it to the road.

The sound of approaching feet drew nearer. To Hardy's surprise, Bud stood motionless, perhaps realizing that in the darkness he was as vulnerable as Hardy. The noise of the LeHew footsteps and their horses seemed to be almost upon Hardy. He was tempted to release the reins and draw his pistol, but he decided to hold tight, not to make any unnecessary movement or noise.

Then Hardy heard a noise deeper in the forest of something rustling through the woods. Maybe it was a deer or a bear, Hardy could not tell, but whatever animal it happened to be, it was a godsend.

"Did you hear that?" yelled one of the LeHews.

"Yeah, let's get them."

With that, the footsteps of the two men quickened, their horses following easily behind them.

Hardy forced himself to count slowly to twenty as the LeHews slid deeper into the forest. Then he started the horses and Bud toward the road, moving as quickly and quietly as he could and wondering when the LeHews would figure out the ruse. In Hardy's mind, the woods reverberated with the noise of their retreat.

Hardy lost track of time and distance. When he thought he should have been at the road, he found no trace of it and began to wonder if he had become disoriented. He halted the horses and Bud for a moment to listen. He could hear nothing over the pounding of his heart. Then he heard Satch LeHew call out.

"They must've slipped past us," he yelled. "Head back for the road and see if we can cut them off. Fire your guns for show."

In succession Hardy heard three distinct shots, but saw no flashes of gunfire. The LeHews were far enough behind him for his plan to work, if only he was headed toward the road.

"Let's go," he said, shoving Bud forward, then leading the horses by the reins behind him. If only the road were near! And, just as he was about to give up hope of finding the road, Hardy emerged onto the hard-packed trail. He hurried Bud down the road toward Boggy Depot, looking for the narrowest place between trees. Finding a spot where he thought it would work, he jerked the hangman's noose from around Bud's neck and grabbed the remainder of the rope coiled around the pinto's saddle horn. He ran to the tree nearest the road and wrapped the noose end of the rope around the trunk, then slid the tail end through the noose itself, drawing it tightly around the tree at waist level. Then he shooed the horses and Bud toward a tree on the opposite side of the road, tying the rope around it and quickly cinching it down.

Catching a deep breath, Hardy yelled as loud as he could. "Mount up, Bud, and ride for Fort Smith, hard as you can." If this ruse worked, the LeHews would hit the trail on the Fort Smith side of the rope. Then he would stampede his and Bud's horses toward Boggy Depot, hopefully drawing the LeHews into the rope.

"Hurry, Bud, dammit," Hardy shouted again as he led the two horses and Bud around to the Boggy Depot side of the trip line.

From the woods came the cry of Satch LeHew. "Don't let them get away. We want the deputy."

Hardy heard the firing of guns. His horses were nervous, stamping the ground and tossing their heads against the reins he managed in his left hand. The LeHews seemed to be approaching the road, all downstream. So far, it was working. Hardy jerked his revolver from his holster and without warning slugged Bud across the side of the head. Bud crumpled on the ground between the horses, further scaring the frightened animals.

Down the road, Hardy heard at least one and maybe all three LeHews emerge from the woods. He released the reins. "Run for it, Bud, they're behind us," he screamed, then lifted his Colt in the air, firing off a shot. The two horses bolted toward Boggy Depot, their hooves thundering down the road.

Instantly Hardy grabbed Bud by his arms and dragged him into the woods as he heard the commotion back down the road.

"They're behind us," Satch LeHew cried. "Get 'em before they get away."

Hardy heard their horses squeal from hard tugs on the reins. Their hoofbeats quieted for just a moment, then picked up as they charged back down the road toward Boggy Depot.

And toward Hardy's tightly stretched rope.

22

Hardy pulled Bud back to a depression in the ground, then ran back to the tree line. The LeHews charged ahead, their mounts' flailing hooves chipping away at the hard-packed road and sending bits of dirt splattering into the trees.

Lifting his pistol, Hardy cocked the hammer and waited. The vibration of the approaching hooves rolled like thunder through the ground as if all three horses were bearing down on him.

His eyes fought against the darkness to make out the approaching riders. Just as he thought he saw a vague form charging through the night, he heard a horse squeal, then heard something pop like a tree limb being broken. A man's scream was drowned out by the thud of a horse landing hard, then flailing and kicking at the ground with its hooves. A man moaned, then cursed.

Before Hardy could sort out the confusion of the first fall, the two remaining horses plowed into the rope. The pounding of the hooves was replaced by the squealing of the horses as their legs were chopped from under them. In the darkness, Hardy thought he saw the form of a horse flipping over on its back. The horse splatted against the ground and a second seemed to fall upon it. The squeal of one horse ended with a sharp crack.

"Son of a bitch," screamed a terrified Satch LeHew. "Jesse, Clyde, you two okay?"

Hardy fired at the noise.

"Dammit, boys, hit the trees," Satch LeHew yelled. "Jesse, you okay?"

"Yeah! What about Clyde?"

Hardy fired at the sounds of the LeHews scrambling into the trees on the opposite side of the road.

"Clyde, Clyde?" yelled Satch. "I think he's dead, Jesse."

The two surviving LeHews fired wildly in the trees all around Hardy.

"I'm not leaving," yelled Jesse, "until Doyle Hardy's dead."

Hardy crawled to the depression where he had hidden Bud. Shaking Bud, Hardy tried to rouse him, but drew only a groan. Hardy considered slipping away into the darkness, but decided against it. Why postpone a showdown with the LeHews and have to worry about them sniping at his back on the return to Fort Smith?

From the road came the noise of two injured horses. One was pawing at the hard pack and whining in pain. The other just whimpered. Hardy wished he could kill them and put them out of their misery, but to do so would risk injury and waste his declining supply of ammunition.

Across the road, he thought he heard one of the LeHews moving among the trees. Crouching, Hardy abandoned Bud and slid some thirty feet along the trees, then squeezed off a shot. Instantly he scurried back toward Bud as the trees behind him were peppered with lead. Hardy screamed, then fell to the ground for effect, hoping that feigning a wound might draw the two surviving LeHews out into the road.

"Did you get him, Jesse?" called Satch LeHew.

"I don't know, Satch. I shot at something moving but I don't know that it was him."

Hardy lay still as calm waters, waiting, hoping that they would cross the road to inspect.

"He's a clever one. He could just be possumin' us, Jesse."

"You want to take a look?"

There was a long pause, the silence broken only by the miserable noises of the injured horses and the slight breeze tiptoeing through the trees.

"Come daylight'll be plenty of time for me. What about you?" asked Satch.

"Doyle Hardy's hard enough to kill in the daylight. I sure don't want to get too close to him in the night."

"Then one of us ought to keep an eye on things while the other gets some sleep," Satch called. "You want first shot at some shut-eye?"

"Don't know I can sleep with those damn horses carrying on."

"You want to shoot them, Jesse?"

Hardy lifted his pistol, taking aim at where he thought Jesse was hiding. If Jesse fired, Hardy hoped to at least wing him.

"I'll pass, Satch, in case Hardy's possumin' us."

Hardy lowered his pistol. It would be a long night, but it was best to settle this affair here once and for all. He just hoped no innocent folks rode by during the night. Most folks avoided night travel in The Nations because of the danger, but occasionally some decent folks were about.

Quietly, Hardy inched back to the depression and Bud. He shook Bud, who groaned slightly, then breathed heavily. Carefully, Hardy broke apart his Colt and pulled each bullet from the cylinder, checking to see if it had been fired. He dropped the empties and replaced them from the dwindling supply in his gun belt. He had a handful more in his pocket, but he had lost most of them pulling his knife from his britches when he had cut down Bud.

Hardy figured he should get a little sleep so he would be alert come dawn and the final showdown between himself and the LeHews. He lay perpendicular to Bud and draped his feet over his prisoner. This wasn't the most comfortable way to sleep for himself or for Bud, but if Bud stirred this would at least wake Hardy up before Bud had a chance to take his gun.

Hardy rested as best he could and the night dragged by so slowly that he was never certain if he had slept much at all. Hardy was awake when the sky began to pale around the edges. He lifted his feet off the snoring Bud. With stealth Hardy eased away from Bud and crawled parallel to the road for about forty feet. He stopped at a half circle of rocks that were further screened by a few pine trees. This would give him good cover. He just wished he hadn't thrown his carbine aside when he cut down Bud. The carbine would've made for a steadier aim.

As the light began to seep over the woods, the carnage on the road became visible. One horse lay on its side still whimpering, one jagged front leg showing bone and the other folded under its chest. A second horse had died across the body of the third mount, its rump sticking up in the air. Sprawled in the middle of the road beyond the horses was the body of Clyde LeHew, his head resting on his left shoulder from a broken neck.

Hardy studied the horses and saw that each still carried the carbine of its rider. Hardy had something to smile about. At least the two surviving LeHews weren't better armed than he. It would be pistols against pistols. Hardy could wait them out. He knew he was unharmed and able to carry on the fight. They didn't know that. It was just a matter of time.

As the minutes passed, the light peeled away layers of shadows that had hidden his enemies and provided cover for Hardy. Shortly, he made out the sounds of men calling to each other in raspy voices that passed for long-distance whispers. He knew they were talking about their strategy, but he could not decipher their words over the distance.

Then on cue, the LeHews began to pepper the woods with their gunfire, concentrating most of their attention on the area where Hardy had fired his final shot last night and feigned a wound. With each shot, Hardy grew more confident that they didn't know his location or his condition. Then Hardy heard a noise to his side and saw Bud rolling over, shaking his head, then shoving his cheek and face into the dirt. For a moment, their gazes locked on each other and Hardy motioned for him to stay down. Bud kept shoving his face into the dirt like a mole. He'd gone damn crazy.

Hardy looked across the road and saw a patch of plaid shirt as it moved behind a tree. Then he saw another man slipping closer to the road, firing as he went. Confident because they had received no return fire, Jesse and Satch LeHew would slip out into the road in a moment to check on Hardy's fate. In trying to determine his fate, they would seal their own. Hardy took aim, knowing full well he must hit each to keep them from advancing on the dead and dying horses to retrieve their carbines. Both men came out of the woods, slowly, tentatively, motioning to each other to advance.

One step, two steps, three steps they advanced, their eyes focused on the spot where they expected to find Hardy's body.

Hardy thumbed back the hammer on the revolver, taking dead aim at the heart of the man in the plaid shirt.

Just as he prepared to pull the trigger, he was startled by a sudden shout.

"Get back, get back," came Bud's unexpected warning.

Hardy fired, missing the plaid shirt of Satch LeHew. Hardy cursed as the two LeHews bounded back into the woods. Hardy glanced to Bud who had worked his gag loose. Bud laughed in triumph.

"Boys," yelled Bud Hardy, "he's behind a circle of rocks on the Boggy Depot side."

"That you, Bud?" yelled Satch LeHew.

"Yeah," Bud answered. "Start shooting, I'll sight you in."

A shot rang out, then another, both moving closer to Hardy.

"Take it south, more to the south," Bud yelled.

Hardy was tempted to shoot Bud, but could not bring himself to kill his own son.

Two shots rang out, one knocking a branch on Hardy's position.

"That's it," Bud yelled. "Shoot lower for the rocks."

The morning exploded with gunshots, pinging off the rocks, whistling through the air, thudding into trees. Hardy ducked his head to avoid the flying rock chips kicked up by the bullets.

Above the gunfire, Hardy could hear a mocking laugh. "Now you're a dead man, Doyle Hardy," taunted Bud. "I'll walk away from here and you won't. These are friends of mine."

Hardy lifted his head as a bullet splattered into the earth beside him, kicking up dirt in his mouth. He spat and cursed. "They're no more your friends than a pair of rattlesnakes."

"How's it feel to know you're gonna die?" Bud laughed. "I'll walk away a free man."

"Not a guilt-free man," Hardy shot back.

The bullets pinged all around him. The LeHews' aim was drawing closer. He must make a move, but where? Bud was the only answer. Anticipating a lull, Hardy lunged from the cover of the rock, hitting the ground at a crouch and dashing straight for Bud, bullets kicking up the dirt behind him. He rolled into the depression with Bud, then grabbed him by the neck.

"We'll see what kind of friends you have, show you what happens when you run with the wrong kind." Hardy released his neck, then grabbed him by the leather thong binding his hands behind his back and pulled him up to his knees. "You boys drop your guns because I'm coming out behind your friend here."

Bud's shoulders sagged. "He's not fooling, Satch," yelled Bud, panic dripping from his words. "You're my friends, aren't you?"

"Sure," shouted Satch, "why shouldn't we be friends with the man who abandoned us in our last fight with Doyle Hardy?"

Hardy jerked Bud to his feet, then wrapped his left arm around Bud's neck and forced him toward the road, gun in his side.

"You boys won't shoot, will you?"

"Why no," answered Jesse, "unless we want to save your pappy the trouble of taking you back to Fort Smith."

Hardy growled in Bud's ear. "Your mother, your father—whoever the hell he is—and a good wife are all the friends you can ever count on in life, Bud."

"Don't shoot, boys, please."

Hardy pushed Bud toward the road, emerging from the woods just as the LeHew brothers came out, broad smiles on their faces. "Drop your guns," Hardy commanded, then grimaced at the sound of the last thing he wanted to hear. By the rumble of the wheels and the rattle of the trace chains, Hardy knew a wagon was approaching from the direction of the Sims's place. He glanced quickly down the road and saw Emma Sims holding the reins and heading in his direction, Hardy's and Bud's horses tied behind. "Drop them," Hardy commanded again.

Instantly, the LeHews lifted their guns and fired. Bud Hardy screamed in terror, then gasped at the reality of death striking his chest. Hardy felt the shudder of Bud's body as the bullets ended his life. Hardy swung around, firing at Jesse, once, then twice more, the final bullet thudding into his chest which turned suddenly red.

Hardy let Bud fall, then swung his gun for Satch LeHew. He must kill Satch LeHew before the bad man injured Emma Sims. He squeezed off his fourth, fifth and sixth rounds to no avail while Satch LeHew squeezed off a single shot which grazed Hardy's left arm.

For a moment, Hardy had Satch's heart in his sights, then he pulled the trigger.

Click!

"Dammit," Hardy yelled.

Satch LeHew smelled the blood of victory. He took aim for Hardy's head.

Hardy had to do something quick or Emma Sims might get hurt or worse.

Satch LeHew thumbed back the hammer on his revolver.

Hardy dropped his revolver and bolted for the horse with its rump—and a carbine—angled up in the air. The sudden movement toward rather than away from Satch LeHew confused him. LeHew fired, missing.

Hardy grabbed the carbine stock and jerked the weapon from its saddle holster. He levered a cartridge into the chamber as Emma Sims drove the wagon straight for the downed horses. If Hardy didn't kill Satch LeHew, Emma Sims would be hurt.

LeHew's confident smile disappeared behind a mask of terror. He shot again. His aim, now beset with a bad case of nerves, was off.

Hardy jerked the carbine to his shoulder and fired.

LeHew stumbled, then righted himself, advancing toward Hardy.

Hardy fired again. The bullet struck LeHew, but he kept advancing as if he were on a mission for the devil. He staggered ahead, aiming his step, if not his pistol, for Doyle Hardy.

Hardy jerked the lever on the carbine, but it was jammed.

LeHew realized the advantage had turned again in his favor. He kept advancing, a smile as wide as Indian Territory on his face. "You're gonna die."

Then an explosion ripped into Satch LeHew. Where once had been a man, now stood a bloody pulp that quivered like a leaf in a gentle breeze, then tumbled over dead.

Things had happened so fast, Hardy did not understand.

He turned toward Emma Sims, but she was obscured behind a cloud of smoke emanating from the barrel of her shotgun.

He shook his head, then threw down the jammed carbine. He twisted around, staring in disbelief at the carnage.

"Why, Bud, why?"

Emma Sims hopped from the wagon seat to the road and ran to Hardy, throwing her arms around him and crying. "We found your horses in our garden at dawn. I feared you were dead." She buried her head in his chest and squeezed against him.

Hardy stood listlessly in her grasp, his own arms limp by his side. Emma was sobbing for him and he could feel her hot breath through his shirt. He could not recall the last time a woman had shown a genuine affection for him. It was a good feeling.

Beyond her he saw the little ones in the wagon, staring wide-eyed at the death upon the road. They were the grandsons he would never have. And the only son he could ever claim was crumpled on the road behind him. He had always considered Bud his son, despite the gossip, and he could have accepted him as son if only Tinnie hadn't poisoned Bud against him.

Lifting his hands, he unwrapped Emma's arms from him and felt her tears upon the back of his hand. She took his hand, lifting it to her face and kissing it gently. He offered her a smile, as best he could, then took a deep breath and turned around.

He walked tentatively to Bud, as if a loud step might awaken his son from a light sleep. For all his time following the outlaw trail, Hardy was still humbled by death, even more so by that of his son. He gritted his teeth and stared at Bud's body, then focused on his face and his still-open eyes. Hardy saw something in Bud that he had not seen in years, a smile, gentle and sincere. It reminded Hardy of the angelic countenances he remembered when Bud was still young and unspoiled by Tinnie's tales of the frontier prince Boone.

Hardy squatted by his son, biting his lip and fighting back the tears. Leaning over Bud, he placed his trigger finger upon each eyelid and closed it. There was nothing more for Bud to see in this life. Hardy hoped there was something beyond the river that would prove a better world for Bud. If his smile was an indicator, then there was such a world.

"I'm sorry, son." And while he now admitted to himself that Bud was not his offspring, "son" seemed the only appropriate farewell.

Hardy felt Emma's hand upon his shoulder and her touch seemed to release the tears welling in his eyes. He felt the tears trickling down his cheeks. He wiped at them with the sleeve of his coat, embarrassed that Emma might see them. He stood up slowly, reverently, looking from his son's strangely placid face to the badge on his chest. His hand rose to the badge and he unpinned it.

Holding the badge before his face, he studied it and shook his head. He had lived up to the oath behind it for years, maybe not to the letter of the law as Marshal Jacob Yoes's rules required, but always to the spirit of the law as he interpreted it. Out in these parts, lawyers, judges and juries weren't around to help a man decipher the law. There was right and there was wrong and a lawman was on his own to decide the difference. Maybe it was the same way with the oaths that bound a man to his honor. Hardy had done everything in his power to live up to his oath as a lawman and it had led to this. He had done everything in his power to live up to his marriage vow and it, too, had led to this.

He slid the badge into his coat pocket. He would never wear it again.

Wiping another tear from his face, he turned around and took Emma Sims in his arms and kissed her full on the lips.

Behind her Hardy heard the sounds of the little ones giggling. Unlike the carnage of the past at his feet, the boys' laughter held the promise of the future.

23

Word preceded Doyle Hardy down the streets of Fort Smith. Everyone wanted to see the lawman who had killed his own son. Folks dropped what they were doing and ran to the walks as Hardy guided Emma Sims's team and wagon down Garrison Avenue, then turned on the street leading to the federal courthouse.

Hardy tried to ignore their stares, their gesturing and their audible second-guessing. They pointed at the back of the wagon where the wooden coffin, the best that could be bought in Skullyville, gave mute testimony to Hardy's no-nonsense reputation. Besides Bud, five men had died on this, his last journey as a lawman into The Nations. The deaths of Flem Thurman, Temp Whitesides and the LeHew brothers added grist to the gossip that Doyle Hardy was the meanest lawman who ever rode in Indian Territory. But the people who told that gossip had desk jobs or sold merchandise or built houses or taught school. They were not men who had taken an oath to enforce the unenforceable.

Hardy scowled at the spectators, then spat on the brick road approaching the courthouse. He reached for the brim of his hat and pulled it lower so people could not view his eyes. As he guided the horses down the drive that led to the front of the federal building, he lifted his head enough to see U.S. Marshal Jacob Yoes standing on the courthouse porch, surrounded by deputies. In an upstairs window Hardy thought he glimpsed the judge himself, Isaac Parker, standing in a blaze of noonday sunlight, his white mane and beard shining in the sun's glare. When the judge had first arrived in Fort Smith, Parker's hair was dark and his stature straight. Now not only was his hair white, but his stance was stooped. Ruling on the law had aged the judge more than enforcing it had aged Hardy.

Glancing down at his suit, Hardy realized how dirty his clothes were. He was embarrassed for the honorable judge to see him this way. When Hardy looked again at the window, the judge had disappeared.

Now Hardy had to face Yoes and answer his questions, then take Bud home and bury him. Yoes stood on the porch, his arms behind his back, his graze inscrutable. Hardy figured Yoes was trying to figure out all the regulations he must have broken in Choctaw Nation. Somewhere along the way Hardy had lost what receipts he had collected, but the receipts no longer mattered. The LeHews' saddles and belongings were piled in front of the coffin while Bud's horse and the homely one Hardy had borrowed from the LeHews trailed behind the wagon.

Hardy swung the team around parallel to the courthouse porch, then jerked on the reins and shoved his foot against the brake lever. As the wagon came to an abrupt stop, curious deputies and courthouse spectators on break for lunch swarmed around it, speaking in whispers and grabbing at souvenirs from the LeHews' belongings. Hardy stood up on the wagon floorboard and twisted around, folding his arms across his chest and staring the crowd into silence. He had no tolerance for the spectators because they reminded him of vultures circling another's kill. Except for the deputies in the crowd, none had the courage to ride The Nations, but each was brave enough to criticize a man who did. Within the coffin rested the remains of the nearest thing he would ever have for a son and these men were prying into his privacy.

The authoritative voice of Marshal Jacob Yoes ended the silent standoff. "You deputies go about your work. The rest of you folks go about your business. Now move."

Grumbling their displeasure at the order, the spectators slowly backed away.

"Hurry up or I'll have you all arrested," Yoes shouted with a sweeping motion of his hands.

Hardy stepped from the wagon box onto a wagon wheel, then jumped to the ground. He stood dusting his coat, ignoring the marshal.

"Sorry about your son, Doyle. I wish it hadn't come to that."

Nodding, Hardy stared at the white pine coffin. There was nothing he could say.

"I hope the word isn't true that you shot him."

Hardy stepped to the wagon, dropping his hands over the sideboards. "I may have killed him, but the LeHews shot him."

"Huh?"

"Truth doesn't matter, Jake, once the rumors start."

The marshal stepped to Hardy's side, his hands

behind his back. "We told Tinnie Bud'd been killed. She never said a thing, Doyle, never asked about you, just stared off into the distance. I got so damn uncomfortable, I rode off without knowing how she felt. She's a hard woman, Doyle, but I figure you know that better than me."

Hardy slipped his hand in his coat pocket where he had deposited his badge. His hand brushed against the tintype of Tinnie that he had taken from Bud's bedroll and he pulled it out with the badge. "I won't be needing this any more," he said, dropping the star into Yoes's hand. He shook the picture, remembering with fondness the Tinnie that he had married and the Tinnie that had stood for this tintype. Shaking his head, he slipped the tintype back in his pocket.

Yoes's fingers clasped around Hardy's badge. "I guess I'll need a final accounting of your trip and an explanation of the horses and the extra saddles."

"The pinto was Bud's so I'm claiming it. The LeHews killed my gray so I borrowed one of theirs, with saddle. I got my saddle and belongings back from their horses after the shoot-out that killed Bud. Without bringing back any prisoners alive, I'm out expenses and out a horse." He was disgusted with the marshal and didn't even turn around at the sound of approaching footsteps.

"You know the rules, Doyle. I'll have to hold the saddles and the horses until the judge can make a disposition."

"The judge has made a disposition," came a voice from behind.

Hardy turned around to face Isaac Parker, himself. "Afternoon, Judge."

Parker nodded at Hardy, then turned to Yoes. "I'm awarding the horses, saddles and any other belongings of the deceased to Doyle Hardy for service above and beyond the call of duty."

"Sir," protested Yoes, "that's not right, not by the book."

Parker answered with a cynical laugh. "No book was ever written that could be followed in The Nations. If we can't serve the letter of the law, we will at least serve the spirit."

"But, sir . . . ," Yoes began.

Holding up his hand, Parker fixed his piercing gaze upon Yoes. "My decision is final so please excuse yourself."

Yoes gave a curt nod and a sigh, then marched back toward the courthouse as Hardy twisted back around to face his son's coffin.

Parker slipped beside him, placing his hand upon Hardy's shoulder. "We're relics, Doyle, you and me. Men like the good marshal and the congressmen in Washington who keep trying to abolish my court think rules can cover everything. You and I know better, Doyle. You and I know that the only constant in The Nations is a good man's word. You're a good man, Doyle. You're a man who sees blacks and whites, rights and wrongs, not all the grays and all the excuses the lawyers see in my courtroom. We're relics, you and me, because we expect a man to live up to his word, to take responsibility for his deeds, good and bad. Every year there's fewer and fewer of us."

"Thank you, your honor."

"No, sir, thank you, Doyle Hardy. Whatever good I've done, whatever order I've maintained in The Nations would not have been possible without your type. I had hoped for a better ending for you and your son. Of all my years on the bench, I've never had a man more dedicated to the spirit of the law. Good luck to you, Doyle, there was never a better deputy in Indian Territory."

Hardy nodded, but found his words blocked by a knot in his throat. Parker seemed to understand, patting Hardy on the shoulder then turning away and trudging back to the courthouse. Observers in pairs and in clumps began to edge back toward the wagon. Seeing the vultures approaching, Hardy jumped up into the wagon, released the brake and untied the reins, slapping them against the rump of the team. The wagon lurched ahead and made a narrow circle before heading away from the courthouse and toward his twenty acres.

People still stopped, stared and pointed along the route, but Hardy urged the team through the sporadic noontime traffic, then headed out of town for home. The team flew through the countryside and quickly covered the distance to his house. As soon as his place came into view, Hardy studied it, shaking his head in disgust. The garden he had worked so diligently was overgrown with weeds. The milk cow in the pen was bellowing from an overloaded udder. Tinnie had done nothing in his absence but likely pine for Boone Dillon or his ghost.

There was no anger at the thought, just remorse, not so much for himself as for Bud. As he drew up to the gate, Hardy spotted Tinnie sitting on the porch in her rocking chair. She barely acknowledged his presence as he jumped from the wagon, opened the gate and climbed back in the wagon. He drove the wagon through the gate and circled around in front of the house. After bringing the wagon to a sudden stop, he jumped to the ground, took off his coat and hung it over the wagon wheel. As he marched to the toolshed, he heard Tinnie.

"Aren't you gonna close the gate?"

Hardy jerked open the shed door and grabbed the same shovel and grubbing hoe that he had used to dig Molina's and Daniel's grave. He strode back to the wagon, stopping about twenty feet directly in front of the porch. He began to dig a grave, a grave Tinnie could not avoid every time she sat on the front porch. Hardy just couldn't see burying Bud beneath the back tree with Molina and Daniel.

"You killed him," Tinnie said.

Hardy glanced up from his shovel. "You killed him, Tinnie, when you turned him against me."

"You weren't his father."

"The law said I was and I would've treated him like my own son if only you hadn't poisoned him against me."

She sneered. "Boone Dillon was his father. That's why I named him Bud for Boone Uriah Dillon, that was Boone's full name. He gave me a child, you only fired blanks."

Hardy nodded. "At least I fired straight. If Dillon gave you a child, he didn't give you a home and security like I did."

"He's coming back to get me. He promised he would. He gave me excitement and treated me like a lady, made me feel more than just a deputy's wife."

"He treated you like a whore, Tinnie." Hardy shook his head and attacked the ground at his feet.

"What are you digging?"

"A grave for your son."

"But it's in the way."

"Do you want to dig his grave?"

"No, no, no," she shouted, bolting up from her rocking chair.

"Do you want his body in your room?"

"No, no," she shrieked, holding her hands to her head, then running into the house and slamming the squeaking door behind her.

Hardy attacked the grave with vigor, anxious to get the job done and then finish his business. Within an hour, he had dug a narrow rectangle that pointed toward the clapboard house. Climbing out of the hole, he speared the shovel into the mound of freshly turned dirt and turned to the wagon, quickly pulling the wooden coffin free, then scooting it along the ground to the end of the grave. Carefully, he slid the coffin into the hole, propping the head against the earthen wall. He slid into the hole and lifted the foot of the coffin, letting the head slide against the wall until the casket's wooden bottom fell onto the dirt floor. He stood on the coffin, then climbed out, pausing for a moment over the grave to say a silent prayer.

That done, he picked up the shovel and began to throw dirt on the pine box. The top of the coffin was still visible when he remembered the tintype in his coat pocket. He retreated to the wagon wheel where he had hung his coat. He shoved his hand into the pocket and extracted the tintype. Returning to the open grave, he tossed it atop Bud's coffin, then began to fill the grave.

When he was done, he threw the shovel and grubbing hoe in the back of the wagon, grabbed his coat and hopped into the wagon, driving it to the toolshed. There he loaded all his hand tools and farm implements. Then he drove back to the house, stopping between the grave and the front porch to gather his other belongings. He bounded onto the porch, flinging open the door and striding to his room. He grabbed the trunk with his clothes and carried it outside to the wagon. As he strode back in, Tinnie stood in the front room, her arms crossed over her breast. She watched without a word as he made a dozen trips to gather whatever belongings were worth taking.

On the last trip he picked up his newest pair of boots, then emerged from his room, pausing for a moment opposite Tinnie. "I'll stop back by town and sign the papers turning the place over to you, Tinnie, but I'll not be back. Ever!"

He strode out he door, tossed the boots into the back of Emma Sims's wagon and climbed into the seat.

"Where are you going?"

"To return this wagon to its owner."

Tinnie seemed bewildered. "But who's gonna farm the place?"

Hardy picked up the reins. "What about you and Bud's father, wherever the hell he is?" He rattled the reins and the team started through the open gate.

He slapped the reins against the team and directed the wagon back toward Fort Smith. He did not close the gate. And, at his last glimpse of Tinnie, neither had she.